"Joanna, I co[...]
me...

"Digging isn't any [...]

"Really? And where [...] up with that notion? In Harrisburg? I have quite a way with a shovel, *denke*," she laughed, trying to put him at his ease.

"Well, I'd certainly appreciate an extra pair of hands now and then," Eli conceded with a grin. "It would help if I knew where to start."

Joanna's stomach flipped at Eli's warm smile. And she suddenly realized she would be spending a lot more time with him over the coming weeks. She couldn't help but be excited at the prospect.

"I'll give it the full three months. See what happens. At this point, I simply don't know," Eli said with a serious face. He held her gaze. "Spiritual fulfillment and a simple life are all well and good. But obviously I hope there might be other benefits as well."

"Like what?" Joanna laughed. "Home-cooked meals and organic vegetables?"

"Nee," Eli said, sobering. "The company of an old friend."

Joanna's stomach flipped yet again.

Hannah Schrock is the bestselling author of numerous Amish romance and Amish mystery books.

AMISH HEARTACHE

Hannah Schrock

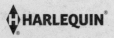 HARLEQUIN®

PLEASE RECYCLE · THIS PRODUCT IS RECYCLABLE

Recycling programs
for this product may
not exist in your area.

ISBN-13: 978-1-335-49911-0

Amish Heartache

First published in 2014 by Burton Crown Ltd.
This edition published in 2020.

Copyright © 2014 by Burton Crown Ltd

This edition published by arrangement with Harlequin Books S.A.

For questions and comments about the quality of this book,
please contact us at CustomerService@Harlequin.com.

Harlequin Enterprises ULC
22 Adelaide St. West, 40th Floor
Toronto, Ontario M5H 4E3, Canada
www.Harlequin.com

Printed in U.S.A.

AMISH HEARTACHE

An arranged marriage was Joanna's worst nightmare until someone from her past showed up in her present.

Joanna Lapp was horrified when her parents announced that they had arranged for her to marry Sampson King. Sampson King, although handsome, was not the type of husband Joanna had in mind. In fact, ever since she was a little girl, she had dreamed of marrying her childhood friend, Eli Stoltzfus, before he suddenly moved away without even saying goodbye.

When Eli unexpectedly returns to Lancaster County, Joanna is confused and more than a little intrigued. It turns out he's not there because of her but because of a memory box he buried all those years ago. She vows to help him find it just to spend time with him again. Soon their childhood friendship turns to adult affection and Joanna knows she's in trouble. She's engaged, after all.

Through misunderstandings, confusion and parents who think they know best, things soon become complicated. Especially when Sampson King finds out that his fiancée has been spending time with the *Englischer*.

Enjoy this sweet Amish romance as Joanna and Eli fight against almost every obstacle imaginable to finally find their happily ever after.

Prologue

8 years ago

At the young age of eleven Joanna Lapp understood the tragedy that had just occurred. She could see it in her friend's tears, in his mother's sagging shoulders and in all of the community as they stood around the open grave.

She watched as Eli Stoltzfus quickly brushed a tear from his eye and wondered why he was ashamed of crying. If she had been watching as her own father was lowered into the freshly dug grave, she wouldn't have been able to stop the tears. She glanced up at her mother who was holding Jeremiah's hand. Jeremiah was only seven, so Joanna doubted her brother understood the true sadness of the day. At seven it was impossible to know what you felt. She remembered it well. But now she was eleven then she understood everything. At least, so she thought.

A yellow daffodil caught her attention in the distance, growing at the base of a tree. Even on a dreary spring morning with sadness and loss surrounding them, *Gott* had sent them a little beam of hope, Joanna thought with a smile before glancing at Eli again. She had always liked daffodils. They told her that winter was coming to an end and spring, with its warmer days, would soon be here.

Ever since her first day of school Eli had been her hero. He was five years older than her, with five years more experience of school and life. They had soon become fast friends when Eli became the teacher's helper. He was always patient with her. Not like the previous teacher's helper who scolded her for not writing her letters properly.

The bishop finished the short graveside sermon, and everyone bowed their heads in prayer. But not Joanna. Joanna turned to look at her friend and prayed quietly that *Gott* would take the place of his father. She knew that *Gott* was everyone's Father, but she hoped He would take extra special care of her friend.

When everyone's heads lifted again her heart clenched when Eli's mother sank to the ground. A group of women surrounded her and helped her up. How terrible it must be for his mother, Joanna thought, clasping her own mother's hand tighter. What had meant to be an ordinary chore had turned out to be the last thing Eli's father ever did.

Later that evening when they returned home, the sadness had followed them. Joanna was on her way to the kitchen to pour herself a drink of water when she overheard her parents talking.

"I don't know how she will survive this. They were so in love, Jared..." her mother's words trailed off and Joanna knew she was talking about Eli's mother.

"*Gott* sends us all challenges, Beatrice, it strengthens us and builds character."

Her mother sighed heavily. "Then I pray *Gott* never sends me that challenge. Did you see her *schweschder* at the funeral? The *Englischer*?"

"*Jah*, I saw her. Came from Harrisburg, I hear. I overheard her ask the bishop if it would be a problem for the widow to come and stay for a while."

"You mean they're going to live in Harrisburg?"

The surprise in her mother's voice mirrored that which Joanna felt. If Eli was going to live in Harrisburg, she would never see him again. She clasped her hand over her mouth; she would talk to Eli about this tomorrow and find out if it was true.

"*Jah*. I understand, though, she needs the financial support her *familye* can offer. Right now, I don't think she's in the right frame of mind to take care of the boy."

"The boy's name is Eli! And he's my friend," Joanna stepped into the kitchen, her outburst turning both her parents' heads in surprise.

"Joanna, were you eavesdropping? You know that is a sin," her father chastened her.

Joanna brushed away her tears and shook her head. "Is it true? Are they going to leave?"

"We don't know yet, honey, at this stage it's all just talk. I'm sure the bishop will make Mrs. Stoltzfus see that the best place for her to be is here, among fellow members of her community."

Her father stepped closer and pulled her in for a hug. "This is a difficult time for all of us, my *dochder*. We need to pull to together in times like these to give strength to the families who have lost their loved one."

Joanna nodded, biting back the tears. "I hope they don't leave."

That night and for the eight nights that followed, Joanna prayed for Eli not to leave. But when he still had not yet shown up at school two weeks later, it was her mother who confirmed her worst fears.

Mrs. Stoltzfus had packed up and left the community without a backwards glance.

Eli Stoltzfus would never be coming back.

The day Ezekiel Stoltzfus died, their community lost not only a valued male member but an entire *familye*. Because some tragedies are just easier to run from than to face up to.

Chapter One

The Conversation

Joanna looked up at the sun in the sky and smiled. It was late March. Joanna had always liked these early spring days the best. More often than not it was still perishing cold, but the winter was now firmly behind them. The evenings were getting longer, and the sun climbed ever higher in the sky with each passing day. The trees were just starting to burst into life, delicate flowers were opening, and the earth sang with the promise of a long and lingering summer.

Joanna brushed the strand of blond hair that had slipped from her prayer *kapp* behind her ear and reached for a hand of soil. The soil was dark, rich with the nourishment the baby seeds would need. She was planting the annual salad crop and her favorite herbs: parsley and chives. She always wondered in amazement how in just a few short months these seeds would grow into strong plants which would then be harvested at the height of summer to feed and sustain the family. Just another of *Gott*'s little miracles that were a constant in their lives.

Of course, even here in the Amish community, the big crops, as she called them, being the wheat and barley, were sown in the open fields by the men using heavy, modern equipment drawn by horses. But here in the garden in front of their little *haus*, Joanna and her *mamm,* Beatrice, were responsible for growing the vegetables that would feed their *familye* the year-round.

Jeremiah, her brother, was no longer a little seven-year-old. At the age of fifteen Jeremiah was learning at his father's hand to be a farmer, like the many generations of boys before them. While Joanna and her mother planted the kitchen garden, Jeremiah and their father were busy sowing wheat. The golden crop provided most of their *familye*'s income, but the vegetables for their sustenance came from their kitchen garden.

Joanna didn't look much like her mother. With a tall frame and blonde hair, she towered over her mother who was petite. Her mother had brown eyes and hair the color of warm cocoa whereas Joanna's eyes were pools of blue. She watched as her mother weeded the garden, bent over with her plain dress hanging in the dirt. Dirt had never bothered Beatrice Lapp. She admired her mother not only for her patience and kindness but for her intuitiveness when it came to the *kinners*. She could only hope that one day she might be half as good a mother as her own.

Beatrice looked at her daughter and smiled with maternal pleasure. *Gott* had granted her beauty, but she was neither vain nor proud. Joanna was nonetheless already nineteen years old. In just a few months she would be twenty and there was still no mention of a potential husband. Many girls were married at a far younger age. Joanna was never short of interest from the boys at the singings, but nothing ever seemed to develop beyond a few buggy rides. Beatrice and her husband, Jared, had been quietly worrying about it for the better part of eighteen months now. To the best of their knowledge their daughter had never shown much interest in any young man and often didn't bother to even attend the singings. As parents they prayed that the right man for their daughter would eventually appear, in the not too distant future.

All Joanna's friends were either married, engaged or courting, but not Joanna. Joanna rather spent her time around the house, tending the garden or cleaning. When Joanna was sixteen, this trait had been endearing to Beatrice, who had been admittedly proud. But the older her daughter became, so her apparent interest in getting married seemed to wane.

"You're dreaming again, *dochder*," laughed Beatrice, breaking the silence. "What do I always say?"

"My head is always in the clouds," shot back Joanna with her own laugh, repeating the words that her *mamm* always used to say when she was a child growing up.

"You know it's true! I'd get your head and feet back on the ground and make sure you sow those chives in a straight line. You know how your *daed* hates things to seem in any way disorganized. He'll have us whip them out and replant them just because they weren't to his perfect standards." Beatrice chuckled. Her husband was a *gut mann*, he cared for his *familye* and helped whenever a hand was needed, but he could be very certain in some things.

Joanna laughed again at her mother's teasing. Her father's love of organization and uniformity were a constant source of amusement to the rest of the *familye*. She loved him unreservedly, but the fact that the books had to be stacked on a shelf in a certain order and the clothing hung in the wardrobe in a specific manner secretly drove Joanna insane. When she was feeling particularly mischievous, she would move an item on the shelf to be a little out of place. The next time she passed it would almost certainly have been moved back to its original position by her *daed*. She knew it was wicked to tease her *daed* in this manner, but she reasoned with herself that there were worse things she could be doing.

Joanna stopped gazing at the scene around her and bent down to continue her planting just as her *mamm* drew closer.

"Your *daed* met with David King last night," she began. Joanna drew a sharp intake of breath; she had a fearful feeling of where this conversation might be headed.

"Why would he meet with Mr. King?" Joanna asked even though she had a very good feeling she already knew the answer.

"Ach, you know *menner*; they like spending time with other *menner*. Anyhow, he went to their *haus*. Very pleasant, he said, they even served him *kaffe* and streusel cake."

Joanna waited, knowing this wasn't really going to be about the quality of the *kaffe* at the King *haus*. "They came to the subject of you not yet courting, and their *seeh* who happens to be in the same situation."

Joanna shook her head. "*Mamm*, please don't tell me *Daed* thought of matching me with Sampson King."

Even though Sampson King was one of the most attractive men in their community, Joanna and he had never been friends. He was tall and broad shouldered, and his eyes reminded Joanna of the young saplings that grew in the woods. Unfortunately, his eyes could just as easily also turn as mean as a feral cat's.

She had her reasons, but they were not to be discussed with her mother. Being taught from an early age that it wasn't her place to judge, Joanna waited for her mother to continue.

"Young Sampson has no mention of a potential *frau*, you know. You're both reaching the age where you need to start thinking about getting married, Joanna."

Although the conversation had not started as such, it suddenly felt more like a speech.

"*Jah, Mamm*," Joanna replied quickly, keeping her head down and engrossing herself in the planting of the herbs.

Beatrice Lapp shook her head at her daughter with a loud sigh. "I don't understand you, Joanna. He's a fine-looking young *mann*, is Sampson, and the Kings are much respected." Beatrice continued, hoping that her daughter would show just the slightest sign of interest.

Joanna kept her eyes on the seeds, ensuring they were sown in a straight line so that her *daed* would not suffer chest cramps due to anxiety, should they show signs of growing all willy-nilly. How was she supposed to react to her mother's suggestion? She had no interest in Sampson King; none whatsoever.

"Joanna," Beatrice pressed, determined not to let the matter rest. "Sampson is a fine, handsome *mann*, is he not?"

"I suppose he is," Joanna agreed heavily. "If you like that sort of thing. Of course, looks should never be a consideration when it comes to the matter of love and marriage. Which is what I'm sure you are really referring to."

"Maybe I am. And of course, looks should not matter, *dochder*. *Gott* teaches us that very clearly," she paused. "But it certainly helps!"

Both women laughed and for a second the tension was broken. "Sampson is the right age for you, Joanna. Unless I'm mistaken, there is nobody else on the horizon for you either. You haven't been attending singings of late and I haven't said this before, but your *daed* and I are beginning to worry."

"You know there's no one else, *Mamm*," said Joanna, looking at her *mamm* sternly, wishing she would drop the matter. "That is why you mentioned it. I'm just not ready for marriage, that's all."

"You are almost twenty," Beatrice replied kindly, reaching out to her daughter's back with a reassuring hand. "You will need a husband soon. You don't want to end up a spinster, do you? He is surely worth considering, isn't he? Just think about the beautiful *bopplin* you'll have. Ach, my *dochder*, I just know you're going to be a fine mother one day." Her mother sighed with a smile and Joanna suppressed the urge to groan.

Joanna had never liked Sampson King. They had attended school together and he would all too often poke her in the back while she was trying to concentrate on the lessons. Then he would have the audacity to deny it when she told the teacher, which simply made Joanna appear foolish in front of the class and had many times caused her to be in trouble with the teacher.

But the real reason she wasn't fond of Sampson King was because of that late summer's afternoon when she was barely eight years old. Even though it happened more than ten years ago, Joanna still remembered it as if it was yesterday.

She had been walking home with her friend Eli Stoltzfus after school. Instead of heading straight home, they had decided to detour through the woods to dip their feet in the cool water of the stream. Once they had removed their shoes and set down their bags, Sampson had crashed through the woods like a young boar on the hunt, smashing saplings to the ground. He had a few kids trailing him who began teasing Joanna and Eli for sitting together on the water's edge.

Suddenly they heard a call of certain despair. Even from a distance, Joanna knew it was the calls of an animal that had been hurt. Being a gentle soul, she jumped to her feet, but Sampson was ahead of the race. His friends followed behind him and Joanna began to fall all the further behind. Eli stayed by her side as they carefully approached once the other kids had come to a stop.

Sampson was towering over a fox trapped in an old snare. The fox's back leg was clearly badly injured as a result of trying to free itself from the snare. Despite having only heard it, it was evident that it had been ensnared for quite a while. He was thin and weak, but anger was clear in the fox's eyes when Sampson dropped the stick on it again.

Joanna knew that foxes were bad for farming, but for the life of her she couldn't remember the reasons as she watched as Sampson tried to put the fox out of its misery with more violence than was necessary.

Joanna hated to see any living creature suffer and she protested, begging Sampson to stop. He just laughed at her. With many of the other *kinners* cheering Sampson on, he wasn't going to stop. Joanna couldn't bear to watch so she turned and ran away, tears flowing down her cheeks. And all the time she ran, she could hear the fox crying out pitifully in anguish like a baby demanding its *mamm*.

Eli had caught up with her, assuring her that the fox had come to a merciful end. He had then brushed away her tears. But the image of Sampson standing over that fox with that stick had remained with Joanna all her life.

Sampson King was nothing but a bully and a brute. Yes, he may have grown into a handsome young man, but it was character that mattered. And in her opinion his character was rotten. Husband material he certainly was not.

Joanna didn't respond to her mother's question. How could she tell her mother about that incident now? Back then she was just glad it was over; she didn't feel the need to tell anyone about it. She glanced at her mother and took a handful of seeds from the bag before carefully placing them one by one in a line. Her mother interrupted her thoughts again.

"Did you hear me, Joanna? Surely you can consider Sampson as a possible match?"

"*Mamm*, do we have to talk about this now?"

Undeterred by Joanna's pleading, her mother continued. "Well, your *daed* believes that he is. He invited the King *familye* to dinner the day after tomorrow," her *mamm* continued matter-of-factly.

Joanna's heart froze. Her parents surely could not be serious? Sampson King? She rubbed her hands together to get rid of the loose soil.

"*Mamm!* I don't wish to be difficult, but I'm not yet twenty. Aren't concerns about me ending up a spinster a little premature?" she sighed heavily. "Please, just take my word for it; Sampson isn't the type of *mann* you want as a son in law. I know *Daed* thinks the world of the King *familye*, but he doesn't know Sampson like I do."

"Can you give us any reason not to like him?" Beatrice asked with a cocked brow.

Joanna shook her head, knowing she couldn't tell her *mamm* what had happened that day beside the stream. "*Nee*," she said softly.

"Your *daed* insists he is," Beatrice insisted, raising her voice. "The arrangements are made. The Kings will be coming the day after tomorrow."

"*Mamm*," Joanna pleaded, standing up to face her, "Sampson King is not a suitable match for me. I've never liked him."

"Then who, Joanna? Who is an option?" an exasperated Beatrice asked with her hands in the air. "Your *daed* and I have given you ample opportunity to find somebody suitable. If you can't find someone yourself, what are we supposed to do? Let you get so old that no young *mann* would be interested? Look at you. You are so pretty. Please don't let your best years pass you by. Do you remember your cousin Rebecca? Rebecca held out and held out, insisting on waiting until she found the right beau…and now?

Rebecca is a spinster at the age of twenty-nine. She has no husband or *familye* to care for. She recently moved in with a widower, just to gain her freedom from her parents."

Joanna knew in her heart that there would never be anybody suitable.

There had been once.

Long ago. But he had left the community suddenly without even bothering to say goodbye. She had known since childhood that Eli was the one. But when he left without saying goodbye it had broken her heart. At the tender age of eleven Joanna had suffered her first loss and, although it was more than eight years ago, she still couldn't imagine meeting a boy as kind or as responsible as Eli Stoltzfus.

"Joanna," her mother reached for her hand and gently enclosed if with her own before meeting Joanna's gaze. "Your *daed* and I have been praying for you to find a suitable *mann*. Then Mr. King asked *Daed* to come and see him… *Daed* believes this is a sign from *Gott,* Joanna. That you and Sampson were meant to be together. We have to follow the path *Gott* has given us, Joanna, otherwise why have we chosen to live by the *ordnung* ?"

A message from Gott? thought Joanna. Could this be really true? It wasn't possible. Surely *Gott* did not want her to be miserable the rest of her life? But Joanna never disobeyed her parents in any way, she wasn't about to start now. She wouldn't refuse to marry Sampson, but she would make sure her parents witnessed his true character before they forced her to marry a man she didn't love.

"If you and *Daed* want the Kings to visit, then of course I will be welcoming," Joanna conceded in a low voice.

If her *daed* believed that this was *Gott*'s will, then maybe it was. Her mind was filled with doubt. She would pray on the matter. *Gott* would tell her what to do, if this was truly His will, then He would show her.

"*Gut*," her *mamm* smiled with great relief. "Let's finish up for today. We can catch up with it later in the week. We had better go inside and do some baking! We have visitors coming!"

Joanna nodded with a heavy heart and wondered what sort of baking her mother had in mind. Whenever they expected visitors, especially ones who didn't come around often, her mother would bake for days on end; everything from cookies, pies and preserves would be freshly prepared. No one would ever accuse Beatrice Lapp of not being a good hostess.

For the first time in her life, Joanna wished her mother hadn't been quite so welcoming.

Chapter Two

A New Life

The sixteen-year-old Eli Stoltzfus watched from the back window of the *Englisch* cab as all he had ever known in life became ever smaller as the distance between himself and his Amish life expanded. It was a long drive. Eli had never been in a motor car in his life before that day. The adventurous experience would have been a great deal more pleasant had the purpose of it not been to drive him all the closer to an uncertain future. When eventually the cab had disgorged them outside Aunt Lydia's home in the city of Harrisburg, he was tired and disconsolate.

Aunt Lydia was Eli's *mamm*'s older *schweschder*. Eli was no longer permitted to use the terms *mamm* and *schweschder*. Tolerance of any and all things Amish was low from the moment they closed the door on the cab that had removed Eli from the simple life. The simple life he had known and cherished.

The simple life in which his precious father had played an integral part. For months, they had lived with Aunt Lydia. It made the transition to the *Englisch* life all the more bearable for the teenager and the mourning widow. They had their own bedrooms, and even had the use of three bathrooms, one with a shower and a bath. And three flush toilets. The house was of course fully electrified, and climatically controlled through central heating, which made the winters decidedly more comfortable. But unexpectedly less convivial. Many was the night growing up in the city that Eli thought fondly back on the years of winters spent around the large black wood stove which had prime position in the downstairs area of their Amish home. It made him sad that he could not share these memories with his mother. The rule was strictly enforced, and his mother's mission clearly set out for them to become *Englisch*. Entertaining any further reminiscences and talk of the ways of the Amish simple life were vehemently quashed. No backsliding allowed!

Aunt Lydia had a daughter and a son of her own. Mary was more than a year older than Eli, and Will was a year younger. Mary had very little time for these Amish relatives. She had a very busy social life, as a senior in her school and a cheerleader. They very seldom saw her, and after the first year she had left Harrisburg and her mother's house to enroll in college in another city. Will was both a great help and a hindering stumbling block to Eli. But Eli well knew that without Will in his new life, he would never have made any kind of life for himself in the strange and confusing *Englisch* world.

It was not long before Eli and his mother moved into their own city apartment, nonetheless within easy reach of Aunt Lydia's house. In no time at all, the mother and son family unit had their very own television and radio, just like any normal family. Eli had been dressed in contemporary clothing and never saw his or his mother's plain clothes again after the first night in the city. He became accustomed to the pop music and talk shows aired on the radio. The radio pumped out its varied offerings from the time his mother woke up in the morning until the television was turned on for the night's viewing when she returned from her day at work. She had landed herself a good job with a printer. Eli had to admit to being awfully proud of the woman he had once known only as a mother and wife. She had convincingly reinvented herself so thoroughly, after having found it impossible to adapt to living the same life as before without her husband.

Eli's transition was less successful. Perhaps his heart had just not been in it as completely as his mother's had been. Perhaps it was just the fact that he was a teenager, thrown so unpreparedly into a world as different from the one he knew as chalk was to cheese. Whatever the reason, Eli adapted with great difficulty. His mother left no room for debate on the matter of his education. He would go to school and he would do the best that he could with the resources at his disposal. Resources that included tools as foreign to him as if he had been expelled from a time machine in a century many years in the future.

It was in this context that his cousin Will played a constructive role. Will had the patience and the enthusiasm to teach him how to use the computer. Will also passed his old mobile phone down to Eli when he upgraded to the newest model available. Will took his responsibility as technical adviser to his cousin very seriously. He claimed that it would have a very bad reflection on him as a modern-day teenager if Eli came across as less than proficient with basic technology. Fortunately for Eli, he landed up in the same class as Will at school. If Eli was grateful to Will for teaching him about mobile phones and computers, then he was forever in his debt for taking him under his wing so graciously in the foreign environment that was the city school. Eli was out of his depth entirely, surrounded by the thousands of children within the confines of the school halls, classrooms, gymnasium, laboratories, playing fields, and school grounds. He was of course a prime victim for the school bullies, the cruel and the misguided. Being largely misunderstood, he was so marvelously open to abuse that it would have been impossible for him to be anything other than a target. Will had to walk a very thin line as his mentor and relation. It was as important for Will to maintain his standing in his social circle as it was to protect his cousin, unwitting alien as he indubitably proved to be. Will chose his battles very well, there was no denying. As such, Eli was not safe from all encounters. But he was always well protected against the worst of the possibilities. He had his moments of being tripped up in the hallways between classes. Once or twice he was bumped surreptitiously in the school canteen and made to spill his lunch on the crowded floor. What undoubtedly followed was the full wrath of the lunch lady, which was regarded as a fate worse than death among the students. The way in which Eli won her over, however, earned him more respect and increased his tally of points among his peers than any sports accomplishment ever could have. There was no denying that his simple upbringing had taught him more than anything else, to be amongst people. To treat others as people in their own right rather than according to any labels ascribed to them by society.

He did well enough at the school subjects, but he excelled in the woodwork class.

"Eli," Will called to him from across the school hallway between classes, "Can you help me out with my woodwork project this afternoon?"

"You explain how it is that 'x' can and does equal 'y' in trinomials and I will do all I can to help you with the woodwork," Eli responded with a smile that lit up his entire face.

Young Milly Jones had been trying to attract Eli's attention since he joined her class that semester, and she figured this line of discussion to be an answer to her wishes. Had she been a praying type, she would have known it to be an answer to her prayers. But she was not. She aspired to becoming head cheerleader as a senior, and she had an innate understanding of figures, but she certainly was not a church-goer. Eli intrigued her. She had never thought that a bible puncher could be quite so affable. But Eli was by far the nicest person she had ever had the fortune to share a space with up to now. She had been looking for the opportunity to get to know him better for some months, and she recognized that opportunity was knocking loudly and persistently at this very moment. She could shy away and possibly lose her one and only chance at getting to know Eli, or she could grab the door handle with both hands and invite opportunity inside.

"I happen to have a free evening, as well as a very good grasp of trinomials and the roles played by exes and y's, if you would like me to explain them to you," Milly extended the not so subtle invitation to Eli.

Eli could not admit to recognizing the young lady offering to help him with mathematics. Will spotted the look on his face and knew without a doubt the turmoil playing itself out in Eli's head as he attempted a suitable response.

"Eli, you remember Milly. She is in our physics class with Mr. Appleby," Will interjected expertly.

Eli was not sure whether it would be polite to feign recognition or better to admit to not knowing Milly. One look at Will's popping eyes and extended chin in Milly's general direction provided the hint he was looking for.

"Of course. Milly. From physics class. Of course, I remember Milly. Thank you, Will," Eli rambled, extending a hand out to Milly. "Eli. Eli Stoltzfus. Will's cousin," he introduced.

Milly smiled widely, both amused and bemused by his response. If he admitted to knowing her, why was he introducing himself, she wondered.

"Hi, Eli Stoltzfus. Pleased to meet you. So, about those exes," Milly batted her eyelids at Eli.

"Exes?" Eli looked to Will for rescuing.

"Trinomials, Cousin. You were looking for help with tying the exes to the y's, remember?" Will prompted encouragingly.

"Ah. Yes. Exes," Eli stammered. "Well, thank you very much, Milly. I would not want to take up your free time, though. You must be a very busy lady out of school time."

Milly seemed at a loss for words at this unexpected turn of events, and so it was that Will once again stepped in to rescue the situation.

"Milly is in the same algebra class as us, Eli. That means she will have to do the same homework tonight as you will have to. Whether she does it alone or while explaining it to you will take the same amount of her time," Will sighed by way of explanation.

Milly decided that the direct approach was called for to get them through this debacle and so she said, "I will meet you at the diner, corner of Elm and Oak, at six. Don't be late and bring your books. Also, enough money for milkshakes."

Eli nodded and Milly turned and retreated to her next class.

"I guess that is a date, then, Cousin," Will shouldered the baffled Eli as he moved off towards his own class.

"Wait. No," Eli called after the retreating Will. "Not a date, is it? An algebra tutorial?"

"If you want it to be a tut class, so be it," Will shrugged and laughed at the confusion evident on Eli's face. "But you don't get out of helping me in woodwork class, so best you get a move on so that we're not both late!"

"A date?" Eli murmured to himself back at his apartment. He would have been a lot more prepared to meet Milly for an algebra lesson than on a date. He was sure Will was wrong about that, he tried to convince himself while trying to decide what to wear to the diner. It had been so much easier dressing as an Amish boy than in the *Englisch* world. He knew what he would have worn to meet Milly for help with trinomials. But what should he wear on a date for milkshakes at the diner, with a pretty, popular girl such as Milly? Eli quickly decided that he was making a mountain out of a mole hill and very definitely blowing the scenario out of proportion. This was not a date. Milly had a good head for figures, and she was simply and very kindly offering to help a less-than astute, struggling mathematician with his homework. She had a very good figure, too, he had to admit. He shook the image of her very good figure out of his head together with the thought.

"Trinomials," he attempted to convince himself again. "That is all it is. An innocent offer of help with my trinomials."

Eli met Milly that evening. He aced his algebra exams that year. And the next. A friendship bloomed between Milly and Eli that never extended to a physical relationship. Despite all attempts by his mother to make him as *Englisch* as possible, Eli could never abandon the Amish view of courting the opposite sex. He had explained his take on relationships to Milly very early on in their friendship, and she had accepted his standpoint graciously. They had nevertheless remained firm friends. It was likely that not taking the friendship to the next level might in fact have made it all the stronger. When time came for them to graduate, Milly had left for New York to continue her studies with the scholarship she had so diligently earned. They spoke to one another often and texted each other even more often. But both knew that they would never be more than the very best of friends.

Milly had long ago realized that Eli's heart belonged to another in his old life back in the Amish community in which he had been raised. She often asked him about his Amish roots and was pleased when he told her that he appreciated having someone he could speak to about that part of his life. She had been sorry to see how upset he was when telling her that his mother did not allow him to talk about that life or the memories he had of his father. She knew that he would return to his Amish life, given the chance.

"What are your plans after graduation?" she had once asked him.

"Despite your very best efforts, I am going to have to lean on my language abilities to see me through rather than my mathematical prowess. I thought I might make a go of journalism."

She had laughed, and they had gone on to discuss his options for college.

"And then once you have your qualification?"

"I don't know yet. Get a job with a newspaper, maybe a magazine? National Geographic would probably love to have me," he had shrugged.

"Where?"

"It's not as if I have a great knowledge of what's out there in the greater USA. If National Geographic want me, though, I'll get that chance at travel and discovery that was always meant to be mine," he had joked, "I had a pretty sheltered upbringing. The more time I spend living the *Englisch* life, though, the bigger the yearning in my heart grows for the simple life my *daed* meant for me to live." He had faltered over the Pennsylvanian Dutch words. Words she had never heard him use before that day.

"Tell me about your father and your Amish life. Would you want to return to that rather than following a career as a journalist?" she had pushed.

"I don't really think I have the option of going

back. I left before I was old enough to be baptized into the church…"

She cut into his explanation, "I was baptized as a baby. How did you get to be sixteen and not yet baptized?"

Despite having lived in the city for two years already, he had never had to explain the Amish beliefs and customs before Milly had asked this question.

"Brace yourself," Eli warned in mock sincerity. "This is going to take a while to explain. The Amish are Anabaptist which simply put just means that they do not agree with baptizing babies. We… They rather favor adult baptisms. Anabaptists believe that following Jesus should be voluntary. They believe that the decision should be made as adults rather than having one's parents decide for you when you are a baby. It is really just a difference in belief systems."

"How do you make the decision, then?" she pressed.

"You get the chance to go on *rumspringa* when you are 16 or 17. This just lets you experience the world outside of the Amish culture and community. It's a period of freedom without being controlled by your parents. Since *rumspringa* comes before you are baptized, you are not yet under the rules of the church. This is so you can get an idea of what you will be missing if you decide to remain Amish. You get to decide on *rumspringa* whether you want to be baptized and live the Amish way, or to leave your community and your family and live the *Englisch* life. Like my mom made me do. To prepare for baptism, the Amish kids have a few months of learning the rules of their church, known as the *Ordnung*, also learning the founding document of Amish belief, the *Dordect* Confession. The *Ordnung* is German for 'order.' It is passed down by word of mouth and gets updated whenever necessary. It also differs from church to church. Youngsters can still change their mind on the day before their baptism ceremony. Those that choose to go through with the ceremony denounce the devil and the world and commit to the church's *Ordnung* and to Christ. The baptism is finalized when the deacon pours water onto the candidate's head through the bishop's hands and gets a holy kiss from the bishop."

"That is quite a decision to make at that age," Milly quipped. "I'm quite glad my parents got to make the decision without involving me," she teased. "What about your father?"

Eli shuffled uncomfortably in his seat and scratched awkwardly at his head. "I decided a couple of weeks after my dad died that I had enough of the grief and pain that his death had caused. I couldn't handle watching my mother dissolve into the sorrow and heart ache any longer. I had to do something. What could I do, though? I was only 16. I hadn't had time to work through my own emotions. I took the little Bible my dad had inscribed for me and buried it inside an oak box together with a piece of his hair and some letters he had written to me when I had been away from home over the years. I buried it without knowing that I would never have the chance to go back and unearth it again. I lost all tangible memories of my dad when I did that. And the worst is that it did nothing to relieve the pain or the heartache of losing him."

Milly leaned over the table and gave his arm a reassuring squeeze. "You will have the chance to rediscover your box of memories, Eli. If you choose to restore that life that you lost through no choice of your own and go back to your Amish community if you ever have the chance to."

"I can't do that to my mother. She has nothing left if I leave her."

"I suppose you are right. It is just a pity that she took the choice out of your hands when she took you away from the Amish life."

Eli could not have known that only four years later, shortly after starting his first job with a newspaper after graduating, that his mother would be diagnosed with cancer.

She had called him into the small sitting room in their apartment as soon as he had come home from work, and he knew that something serious was in the air.

"Eli, I may have made a mistake taking you away from your father's family and your heritage."

"You made the right decision at the time. It is not for you or me to dispute it now," Eli had assured her, surprised by her admission at that late stage.

"I just want you to know that you do have fam-

ily still. That you don't have to live the rest of your
life knowing only Aunt Lydia and your two cous-
ins here in Harrisburg. Now that we have that out
in the open, I went to see the doctor last week. He
ran a few tests, the result of which came back this
week. We have double checked the results, so there
is really no doubt at all. I have cancer. It's not too
late for them to treat it, though, so we are not without hope," she rushed to explain.

Eli had dropped to his knees beside her chair
and now held her tightly. She had kept her com-
posure despite his reaction and moved him to face
her once more.

"You know that you can still go back to your father's family, if that is what you decide."

"Mom, I'm not going anywhere. I belong with
you and that is final."

Two summers later, despite the treatment having
done its job over the earlier months, the cancer had
spread out of control and Eli had buried his mother
in the little graveyard near Aunt Lydia's house in
Harrisburg. While his mother had been fighting the
disease, he had been head hunted by another newspaper in the city. Now that he was alone in the world,
with only his career as his lifeblood, he had been offered the promotion to investigative reporter. But he
was not ready to pour all of himself into his job. He
had been thinking about that little oak box, buried
in the woods near the house that he had been raised
in as a child. An Amish child. He had to find that

box. That box held the answers to the questions he was starting to ask himself in the dark hours, when he was all alone in the apartment his mom had once shared with him. He knew now that he had chosen to do away with those items in the heat of the moment, as a young teenager, newly bereft after the death of his father. Had his mother not moved him away from his home without warning, he knew in his heart that he would have unearthed that hidden box soon after he had buried it. He knew that he would have come to his senses and made a plan to have the tangible memories of his beloved father where he could touch them and feel them whenever he needed to.

Without even thinking about it, Eli fished his mobile phone out of his pocket and pressed the contact labeled as Milly. It hardly rang before she answered with: "And to what do I owe this honor, Mr. Stoltzfus, Sir? Are you looking for a lead to a story that only I can help you with?" she teased, just as she always had even when they were teenagers.

"You know you have always been the only one that could ever help me, Mrs. Iverson. How is married life treating you now that the honeymoon period is long gone?"

Milly had married her college sweetheart, a law graduate, Trever Iverson. She now lived in New York, plying her trade as a forensic accountant.

"Well, it's too late for us, now, Eli. I am expecting Trevor's baby in the fall," she laughed.

"That's wonderful news, Milly. Congrats. Why did you not let me know?"

"Your calculations have just never improved, have they? If I am due in the fall, that means I could only just have found out I am expecting, Eli," she reproved him playfully. "In fact, besides the father and our parents, you're the first to hear the news from us."

"Now I am the honored one."

"Unless you are hiding psychic powers, though, this is not the reason for your call. Is everything alright?"

"Perfect. I have been offered a promotion at work. But first, I am going home to do some long overdue digging…"

"Home? As in Lancaster County home?" she held her breath.

"The one and the only," Eli laughed. "You have a good memory along with that mathematical brain."

"What brought this on, Eli?"

"Now that I don't have to concern myself with my mother, I can fill that hole that leaving my father's family left in my life. I think that if I can get back to where I started, I might find the answers I have been looking for over these many years. If not, I still have my job in Harrisburg. They are letting me off on a sabbatical."

"You're sure, Eli?"

"I am sure that I don't belong here, Milly. I may not be sure of anything else. But that much I can pretty much vouch for. I haven't burnt any bridges, so I can pick up this life if that's what comes of my trip down memory lane. If I don't go, though. I will never know."

"Well. Eli, I wish you the very best and I hope that you do find what you are looking for. And I don't mean the buried treasure. I mean whatever it is that has been missing from your life since you moved to Harrisburg. You deserve it all, Eli. I hope you find it, or it finds you. Either way, I want to know. Keep me in the loop, you hear?"

"You just try to stop me," Eli retorted and disconnected the call with the perfunctory salutations.

Chapter Three

Returning to the Past

Eli Stoltzfus sweated as he lifted the axe for the hundredth time that morning. He brought it down, splitting the thin log in two. He was breathing heavily, and his right arm felt ready to burst; he wasn't used to hard physical work such as this.

For the past eight years, the closest Eli had come to physical labor was climbing the two flights of steps to his apartment. Even though he had frequented the gym in his building, no machine could simulate the benefits of manual labor. Especially under the watchful eyes of an uncle only feet away, making sure you could still handle it.

He wiped the sweat from his brow and glanced out over the rolling hills of Lancaster County and wondered if he had done right by coming back. He enjoyed the hard work and he enjoyed the fresh air even more, but he didn't know if manual labor would bring him the answers he needed.

Eli could still remember the day they had left. He had looked out the cab's back window and cried. His mother had taken him away from everything familiar; from his family home, his friends, and most of all she had taken him away from Joanna Lapp.

Since his return to Lancaster County the week before, Eli hadn't managed to gather the courage to go and see her as yet. It had been eight years since he stood by the graveside as they lowered his father into the ground. So much could have happened in eight years. Joanna could have courted and married, for all he knew. She might already have her first child. It wasn't strange for Amish girls to marry at seventeen and already be a mother by the age of eighteen.

His heart squeezed in his chest. Who would she have married? Eli remembered most of the boys in the community and none of them seemed a suitable match for his best friend. He could still remember her big blue eyes and honey-blonde hair, and the smile that brightened even the darkest day.

He lifted the axe again and brought it down with force. The sound of splitting wood cut through the air moments before the logs dropped to the ground. For the last eight years he had called Harrisburg his home. When they first moved to the city, they had lived with his Aunt Lydia for a while before his mother got them their own apartment. Since that day it had been his mother's mission for them to become as *Englisch* as they could possibly be.

She had installed a television and a radio was always playing in the kitchen, and soon their plain clothes were set aside. Just like the memories of his father that they were no longer allowed to mention.

In his heart Eli had never become *Englisch*, as his mother now was. For the last couple of years something had been tugging at him to return to Lancaster County. Eli wasn't sure what it was, all he knew was that he thought about his Amish childhood now more frequently than ever before.

He had prayed for guidance from *Gott* about the situation, but as an answer *Gott* had only brought him more memories of the Amish community. The simple life of chores to be done and adhering to your faith. The way everything was centered around community and religion. Many people would scoff at a life like that, but for Eli it was the best life ever.

Finally, Eli had done what he never though he would do ever again. He contacted his uncle, Jacob Stoltzfus. In the years since he left, Eli had written to his uncle every now and then to find out how they were doing, but in his last letter he asked a favor. He asked a favor that might bring discord to the Stoltzfus family in the community and more… it might cost Eli his job. But it was something that he needed to do.

He requested permission for an extended visit and fully expected his uncle to object. Eli wasn't Amish, he wasn't even baptized. For all intents and purposes, he was *Englisch*, but that didn't stop Jacob from welcoming him.

It took him a little more than a week to sort matters out in the city before he drove to Lancaster County. Eli had never felt more at home than when he stepped out of his car and smelled the clean farm air.

"Hard work, isn't it, boy?" shouted Jacob as he emerged from the *haus* armed with two white porcelain mugs of *kaffe*. Jacob was his father's *bruder*, although they looked nothing alike. His father had been a short, thin *mann*, whereas Jacob was tall and broad. But they both had that same infectious smile that immediately brought joy and warmth to those around them.

Eli chuckled, setting down the axe. He briskly rubbed his right arm before letting it hang by his side. "I had forgotten how hard it was. I can't remember the last time my muscles quivered from exertion, but I'll get used to it again." He moved towards his uncle who held a cup out to him.

"Here my lad, drink this *kaffe*. It will give you a kick. You don't want to lose a finger with that axe, do you? I'm sure you had *kaffe* in the city, but I'm equally sure it wasn't half as good as this. Remember old Levi? He roasts his own beans now, makes quite a difference," Jacob chattered on, but Eli didn't mind. After being away for so long he liked catching up on the rest of the community and what they had been up to while he'd been away.

"Of course," Eli said, nodding his head as he took the cup from Jacob's giant hand. He grinned to himself as he remembered how his mother could never get out of the habit of saying *kaffe* instead of coffee, even after years in the *Englisch* world. As such, he often used the word himself. His mother had become *Englisch* in all other ways that mattered. She only wore *Englisch* clothes, she was engaged to an *Englisch* man, and the only thing reminiscent of their Amish life was the handmade quilt that covered her bed.

Eli thought back to his typical early morning routine back in the city. A routine that centered around one place—Starbucks. He would sit in the same booth each day, his skinny cappuccino and the morning newspaper in front of him, counting the number of stories that had actually made it to print. Seven was his record. He would normally drink his way through two cups before making his way to the newspaper house. It was in that coffeehouse, watching the chaos of the outside world unfold in front of him, that Eli began thinking about his life. It was in that little Starbucks booth that he worked out the reason for his discontent. It was also where he realized something was pulling him back to the Amish community.

More and more, Jacob began thinking of the Amish way of life.

A simple life.

A life where wealth, pride and vanity didn't exist. A life where having the right relationship with *Gott* was most important. Eli had clung to his religion after their move to the city, but he often found himself wondering if it was truly faith if you only tended to it for an hour once a week.

In Lancaster County faith wasn't a once a weekly appointment. In fact, because of the distances between farms, church services were only held every fortnight. But the Amish didn't need a church to serve their *Gott*. No, they served Him in everything they did. From the way they tended their livestock, to the way they tended their fields. It was hard work and a simple life, which Eli couldn't help but miss now that he was growing older.

Wouldn't it be better than the daily quest for wealth and riches that the *Englisch* always seemed to be in pursuit of? For years Eli had been chasing his own dreams. Becoming a journalist had been his passion since their teacher told them that journalists held the world in their hands with their words.

Powerful words to a teenager searching for purpose after his father's untimely death.

But that wasn't all that was drawing him back to Lancaster County. Somewhere at the edge of the forest, buried beneath the rich dirt, lay his box of treasures. Was that the reason Eli wanted to come back? Maybe if he found that box of treasures, he would manage to put some of his own demons to rest.

After a little over three years as a journalist, his editor had told him he was going places. The problem was not knowing where he wanted to go. He was offered a promotion as an investigative journalist following stories around the country.

With the chance to see the world, all Eli could

think of was seeing his childhood home again. It was in that moment that he realized that he wouldn't be able to move forward with his life until he somehow managed to lay the past to rest.

Instead of thanking his editor for the opportunity, he had asked for a three-month sabbatical. He could still remember his editor's shocked expression. In exchange for his sabbatical he promised his editor a detailed series of articles about the Amish way of life.

Excited and eager for new material, his editor had finally agreed.

But Eli had no plans to betray his community by offering their life stories in exchange for payment.

No; his reasons for coming to Lancaster were completely different.

He wanted the chance to see old faces, he wanted his box and he wanted his demons to disappear. Most importantly of all, he wanted to see if there was a chance for him to be happy. Because ever since driving out of Lancaster in that cab, on to Aunt Lydia's in Harrisburg, happiness had absolutely eluded Eli. The small empty hole in his chest seemed to have grown with the years and was now a large gaping pit of sadness and uncertainty about his own future.

The *kaffe* had a strong kick and a bitter taste that caused him to screw his face up in mild shock. "I see there's no change with the *kaffe*, then!" he joked with Jacob. "This stuff could still wake someone from the grave."

Jacob laughed, shaking his head. "Nothing has changed, boy," Jacob smiled. "We are Amish! Remember? Everything is constant."

Eli remembered a great deal. Sometimes he thought that was why happiness eluded him.

He remembered his childhood; how in love his parents had been. He remembered the plain two-bedroom cottage they had called home. The kitchen garden and the early nights. The wood stove in the kitchen providing heat and sustenance to their family.

His father's bible providing *Gott*'s word and guidance to the family. He remembered the cold winters, snuggling up with a cup of *kaffe*; the warm summers and the cool streams. He remembered unbridled joy; he remembered happiness that didn't depend on success.

He remembered an easier time.

His life in Harrisburg had never come even close to duplicating what he had in Lancaster County. In a question of months, he and his mother were both caught up in the expectations and demands of the *Englisch* world. Their Amish roots long forgotten.

Eli remembered his small school and he remembered Joanna Lapp. He remembered how he had taken to her already on that very first day when she had looked at him with tears in those pools of blue. He remembered her happy laughter, her sunny disposition and how a girl four years younger than him became his best friend.

And of course, he remembered that fateful day

when he came home from school to find a row of buggies beside their barn. He remembered the scent of daffodils and freshly turned earth as he walked into the house filled with people.

His mother had been seated in the chair where his father always sat, but that wasn't what caught Eli's attention. What caught his attention was the sullen looks on all the faces present. The tears streaming over his mother's cheeks and the look of despair in her eyes.

Confused and more than a little afraid of what might have happened that morning while he'd been learning to do math, he had walked to his mother. Without saying a word, she had framed his face with her hands and the grief in her eyes had said everything.

His father had left early that morning to repair the King's barn. The last hailstorm had shown up a few leaks in the roof and no one knew better how to fix a barn roof than his father. A skilled carpenter and respected by the community, his father's services had been summoned.

But what should have been a routine job turned hazardous when a light summer shower began to fall. It was that light summer shower that caused his father to lose his footing and tumble to the ground.

It was quick, the bishop had explained. Painless.

But all Eli could remember was the pain gripping his heart in such a stronghold that it felt as if a vice had been twisted and his heart was about to burst. He tried to find solace in the knowledge that his father had felt no pain, but it was difficult since Eli couldn't seem to get rid of his own pain.

The home that was once happy was now sad and empty.

His *mamm* was restless in the days after the tragedy, and she never seemed to sleep. If Eli stirred in the night, his *mamm* would always be awake, reading her bible or quilting—always the tears flowing silently down her face.

It wasn't long after that he arrived home from school to find their bags packed and a cab waiting. His mother's explanation made sense at the time. But now, looking back, it didn't make sense at all.

"We need to get away from the sadness and the memories, Eli, that's the only way we'll find happiness again."

But Eli didn't find happiness again. He found himself in a strange city filled with people; people who didn't care about an Amish teenager who had just lost his father.

Eli had learned in the years since that fateful day that it didn't matter how far you tried to get away, your memories will always take you back. Maybe that was why he needed to come back. He needed to make peace with the past before he could look to the future. He needed to find a way to fill the hole in his heart.

When his mother passed away the summer before from cancer, that hole only seemed to expand. It was as if everything came rushing back and the only time Eli felt truly calm was when he remembered his home.

Eli planned on staying with his uncle for three months, but after barely a week he already wondered if he would ever be returning to the city.

Jacob and Delia had no *kinners* of their own. They had been blessed with a daughter who would have been around his age as him. Eli had never known her. She died of a fever when Eli was still a baby. The fever had gripped the whole community that cold, dark winter. The young, the old and the weak dropped like flies. Eli had also contracted the fever, yet he survived while his cousin had been taken by it.

For some reason he had always felt guilty about this. Eli found it strange that *Gott* could take one child yet spare another for no reason fathomable to man. When he looked into Delia's eyes on his arrival the night before, he could still see the pain behind them. The loss of a child would never heal, he guessed.

Jacob sat down next to him on the smooth rock he always used as bench in front of the shed. "It will take you time to adjust, Eli. Life is still so very different here," he said while sipping his own *kaffe*.

"Probably," agreed Eli. "But it's so peaceful, so serene. The city is just so busy. Fast paced. Everyone looking out for themselves, always doing what will benefit them and not others. Everyone seems to be chasing fame, personal gain and fortune instead of realizing that their happiness lies within their grasp if they just look to *Gott* instead of their bank accounts."

His mind jumped back to the newspaper office and the backstabbing and constant attacks between fellow journalists as they all attempted to outdo one another.

"These last few months, ever since *Mamm* died, I have found myself remembering more and more about life here. Simplicity, it seems like a blessing. Will I be able to adjust, Jacob? I don't know. But I have three months until my job disappears for good. Hopefully by the end of three months I'll know what *Gott* has planned for me."

Jacob nodded, "Eli, you are always welcome here, and you can stay as long as you desire. You know that." He took another long drink of his *kaffe*. "You know I can see a lot of my *bruder* in you. You resemble him greatly."

"Do I?" asked Eli inquisitively, putting down his own *kaffe*.

Jacob nodded, a faraway look coming into his eyes as he spoke of his brother.

The subject of his *daed* always intrigued him. He had been just a boy when his father had passed away; a boy at the edge of manhood. And yet over the years the image of his father had begun to fade, recollections of his voice had disappeared, and the only thing Eli could still remember clearly were his father's kind eyes.

"I have to say I can barely remember what he looked like." Eli always regretted not having pho-

tographs of his *daed*. But of course, photographs
were not permitted in the Amish community. This
rule aimed to promote self-modesty. It is also one of
the commandments in the bible. The Amish's deep
belief in the stricture that the bible prohibits graven
images to be made of oneself comes from the second of the ten commandments. When Eli had asked
his *mamm* as a boy why they were not permitted to
have photos, she had sat him down and read him
the bible scripture. Verse four in Exodus 20 is very
strictly adhered to: "You shall not make for yourself
an image in the form of anything in heaven above or
on the earth beneath or in the waters below."

She had explained how the bible taught how *Gott*
made man in His image. For this reason, he had
come to understand, it was a form of idolatry for
man to create any physical representation of himself. A photo would therefore limit the perception of
what *Gott* is really like and in that way also damage
the relationship with Him. Eli would nevertheless
have very much appreciated a photo of his father so
that his image did not have to fade in his memory.

"Tell me what my *daed* was like."

Jacob's eyes began filling with their own tears
as he thought about his older *bruder*.

"He was very kind, always looking out for me
when we were growing up. Whenever I faced a problem, your *daed* was there to help me solve it. When
the other boys were cruel, he would take them to the
woods and when they came out, they would never
be cruel again. His belief was very strong. He knew

he had purpose. Your *daed* was the *mann* I try every day to be. He was a *gut mann*, Eli; you should be proud of that."

The picture came to Eli's mind of his father's coffin being gently lowered into the hand-dug grave. No flowers. No hymns. It wasn't the Amish way. The bishop spoke for what seemed like hours. The young Eli stood patiently by the graveside when all he wanted to do was run away. He hadn't visited the grave since his return, but he knew visiting his father's grave would help him put the past to rest.

Not for the first time did he regret burying that box all those years ago. He guessed he was angry at the time. Angry at his *daed*, who had left him without saying goodbye. Angry at *Gott* for calling him to Him so soon. Two weeks after his father's death, seeing his *mamm* awash with grief, Eli had filled a small oak box with his little black Bible inscribed by his father in the cover, a handful of other letters his *daed* had written him over the years, and a lock of his father's hair. He then rushed out to the woods with a shovel and buried it. As if he was burying his own grief and pain.

The very next day he came home from school to find his *mamm* waiting outside next to a cab, their sparse belongings already packed. She had explained what was happening without giving him a moment to object. Although Eli was sixteen and could have insisted on staying in the community, he couldn't stand to see his mother face the pain and loss alone. He had glanced over his shoulder at his childhood home and accepted that he had to go with his mother. She was suffering more than he was and he needed to look out for her.

He had followed her to the cab and bid farewell to everything and everyone he knew.

Jacob could see the pain in his nephew's face and tried to lighten the mood. "Look boy, its *gut* to have you back, whether it is just for three months or for *gut*, that choice is yours. But in the morning, there is one thing that we have to teach you."

Eli frowned. He could do everything Jacob had asked of him during the few days he had returned. "What is that?"

Jacob shrugged with a teasing smile. "You gotta learn how to drive the buggy—I'm not driving you around for the next few months. You can go straight on back to the city if you want a chauffeur—is that what they call it?"

"*Jah*," Eli laughed. "I'm not afraid of driving the buggy, I'm afraid of the horse. I don't think I've touched a horse since *Mamm* and I left."

"Our gelding is a kind horse with a gentle disposition. Only kicked me twice."

Eli chuckled, knowing his uncle was kidding. "You'd better tell that gelding I kick back."

Jacob stood up and collected their mugs. "I'm heading that way now. Why don't you finish up and then we'll go see what your aunt decided to make us for dinner? You know she makes a mean liver stew."

Eli cringed at the words but forced a smile. His uncle had a wicked sense of humor and he often couldn't tell when he was joking and when he was being serious. He picked up the axe and continued to split logs. It might be early spring but there was cold to come yet and the next winter was only six months away.

If there was one thing every Amish person knew it is that you could never have too much chopped wood.

Uncle Jacob and Aunt Delia had refused payment of any sort for his keep, and Eli knew how much an extra mouth to feed would cost them. The least he could do for room and board was to make sure they had enough wood.

Before he dropped the axe again, he glanced into the distance in the direction of where Joanna Lapp had lived as a child. He didn't have the courage to pry about her with Uncle Jacob but perhaps he would run into her in town, or better yet, perhaps he could go and see her.

A smile tugged at the corners of his mouth at the thought. Seeing Joanna Lapp was going to be the best part of visiting Lancaster County; that was if she wasn't married yet.

Chapter Four

Raising

Three days after their conversation in the garden, Joanna and Beatrice stood at the trestle tables beneath an old oak tree. They, along with a few women, were preparing the noon meal for almost the whole community. It was a busy day but one that always brought joy to their community.

Buggies lined the drive of the Miller farm, children were playing hide and seek in the garden whilst the men were working on the barn. The scent of lumber, hard work and good food hung in the air.

Today was the first barn raising in two years. The entire community was as excited as the Millers. Whenever a barn raising took place, it always surprised Joanna how the community would come together, not only with helping to pay for the lumber, but to pitch in with the hard work that was required.

But that wasn't the only reason Joanna was smiling as she made the garden salad. The true reason for her smile was relief. On the day the King family were supposed to come for dinner, word had been sent that the entire family had the flu. Unfortunately, Sampson had gotten the worst of it and was bedridden.

Although she knew it was wrong, Joanna couldn't help but be delighted! Her *daed* moaned quietly in his chair, while Beatrice glared at her daughter once or twice to make sure she wasn't smiling too much when the news came.

Later that evening when her *daed* had gone for a walk and they were alone, Beatrice told Joanna, "This isn't an end to the matter, you know. He is still very set on the idea."

Joanna let it pass. The visit had been delayed, for that she was grateful. When the subject was raised again, she hoped she would have a suitable objection. But for now, she was safe, and life would continue as before.

She also knew that her *mamm* was right. Her father wouldn't let it be; he would wait until Sampson was healthy and invite them to dinner again. Over the last few days Joanna couldn't help but wonder what she could do to make sure Sampson wasn't interested. Her thoughts had lightened her mood even more.

She wanted to have a family of her own one day and she wanted a husband who loved her, but in her heart, Joanna knew that Sampson was not that man. She couldn't bear the thought of being tied to him for the rest of her life. He was a mean person who gained favor with everyone by pretending to be someone he wasn't.

A smile crept onto her face at the thought of him being ill. She had prayed for *Gott* to heal him, but she didn't pray for *Gott* to make his recovery speedy. She knew it was wrong, probably terrible of her, but she also knew her father. He wouldn't rest until she stood in front of the bishop with Sampson at her side.

"Joanna, how far is that salad?" her mother suddenly asked by her side.

Joanna smiled, "About two feet from you, *Mamm*."

Her mother rolled her eyes, "Good heavens, at the rate you are slicing tomatoes they'd be lucky if they had their salad by midnight."

Joanna laughed, "Don't worry, *Mamm*, I'll speed it up."

She took one last glance as one side of the barn was lifted and then she focused on the task at hand. At a barn raising everyone worked, and everyone worked hard. But the men were usually famished by lunch time. Joanna couldn't help but admire them as they hauled lumber and climbed over the wooden structure as if they were born to it.

It was truly a sight to behold, one that always fascinated her. She slid the sliced tomatoes into a salad bowl and began on the onions.

Outside, Eli stood awestruck watching the spectacle unfold before him. It was not yet noon but already the frame of the giant barn was raised, and half a wall was in place. He had seen a few barn raisings as a child, but at that age he simply didn't appreciate the speed and precision at which the men worked. Every man in the community knew his role in the raising and was an expert at it. Every man, that was, apart from Eli.

Before his father passed away, he had taught Eli a few things about carpentry, but not nearly enough for Eli to be called a carpenter. His Uncle Jacob had shared his father's love for carpentry and was still the best carpenter in the community today.

Eli offered to help a few times, but Jacob's words had been firm. "Better to stand aside than to help and be in the way."

He couldn't help but feel slightly offended by his uncle's words, but he understood. It had taken months of planning for this barn raising. Detailed planning was involved for every step of the day, every man assigned to a job. He would just be in the way.

Just like he was when he was a child. This was Eli's third barn raising. The first time he had just started school and was kept as far away from the barn and the lumber as his mother could manage. The second time Eli had been about twelve years old. His father had planned that barn raising. He could still remember months of meetings and planning. He also remembered the way everyone looked to his father for guidance. Eli couldn't imagine anyone looking at him with that kind of respect.

After spending eight years in the city Eli appreciated more than ever before the skill that went into raising a barn in a day. In the city everything was about money; wages by the hour, permits and politics. Here, things were simple.

If someone needed a barn after theirs was ruined by a storm or fire, the community stood together. The planning and management wouldn't cost the owner in excess of a year's wages. The labor, the food, and even the lumber was donated for the occasion. Eli scuffed his boot in the dirt. He couldn't imagine people offering all that for free in the city, not where everything was about wealth and status.

In recent years barn raisings had become less and less. Not only because of the shortage of skilled carpenters in every community but because of the dwindling number of working farms. Some Amish folks now took *Englisch* jobs in towns; others would work at factories to earn their weekly wage.

But when it happened, it was a miracle. *Englischers* that drove past stopped at the side of the road aiming their phones at the quick construction and skilled craftsmanship. The fact that all the men worked together meant that the structure grew effortlessly—in the *Englisch* world this sort of project would take days, if not weeks, and of course everything would be geared up for maximum profit.

"Could you get more nails from the workbench in the front?" a man Eli didn't recognize called out. Eli nodded and headed towards what he figured was the work bench. A few trestle tables had been set against each other to offer a large working space. He located the nails and headed back around the pile of lumber to hand it to the man.

Eli tried to put names to faces but failed the majority of the time. He had been away a long time and age had taken a toll on many of the men.

He moved a few paces from the structure, making sure he wasn't in the way when suddenly he felt a hand on his shoulder. "Eli Stoltzfus?"

Eli turned around and his eyes narrowed in confusion. The man looked familiar but again he failed to put a name to the face. "*Jah*, that's me."

"Bishop Raber." The gentle blue eyes were almost translucent with age, his silver hair mere wisps in the wind.

"*Jah*, I remember, my *daed*'s funeral…"

"That's right," the bishop smiled, and Eli felt a nervous tug in his belly. He knew that Uncle Jacob would have needed permission for Eli to come and stay and suddenly wondered if he was welcome at the barn raising.

"I'm glad you've come home, Eli. We were all very sad the day you and your *mamm* left. How is she?"

Eli swallowed past the grief that still caught him off guard sometimes. "She passed. Last summer. Cancer… At least she's no longer suffering."

The bishop nodded in understanding. "She walks with *Gott* now, and with your *daed*."

A ghost of a smile played on Eli's lips. "That's

what I tell myself every day. If my being here isn't appropriate... I'll go back to Jacob's *haus*."

The bishop chuckled, "Why wouldn't it be appropriate? You were once very much a part of this community. I'm happy you decided to come and visit with Jacob and Delia. Three months, he said?"

"That's right. Three months for now..." Eli trailed off. He still hadn't decided how long he was going to stay or what he would have decided after the three months.

"Maybe you'll come and talk to me before then. I can't just baptize you, Eli. Surely you understand that. We'll have to look at a proving period of some sort or something like that."

Eli frowned, "I don't know if I'll be staying. It's just a visit...for now."

The bishop nodded with a knowing gaze. "I look forward to having that talk with you, Eli. Sometimes in the most unexpected places you find what you didn't realize you need. I don't think you would have come back to Lancaster if you didn't feel there was something lacking in your life. You're welcome at Sunday service for as long as you're here."

The bishop turned and walked away leaving Eli staring after him. He wasn't sure what had just happened, but the bishop was right. He was here because he couldn't find happiness, because something drew him back to Lancaster after his mother's passing. Eli just wasn't sure what that was just yet.

He glanced at the structure again. All four sides had been lifted and the men were attaching the sides while others were starting to nail in the roof shingles. Eli was proud to see that Jacob was at the center of today's raising. He was a master carpenter and the men obeyed his direction. But seeing him on the apex of the structure without safety equipment brought a tight knot to his stomach. His *daed* had plunged off the top of a barn just like this. It would be too much for history to repeat itself.

He swallowed past the fear and sent up a quick prayer for *Gott* to protect his uncle while he was working on the roof shingles. Sometimes the *Englischers* had a point, he mused, thinking of the harnesses and helmets that would have been protocol in the city.

But this wasn't the city. This was Lancaster County. This was where things were still done the way they had been done in previous eras. Accidents happened and you could try your best to prevent it, but at the end of the day when *Gott* called you home, no equipment or precautions could stop Him.

Jacob hammered in a final nail and then called an end to the morning's work as he climbed skillfully down. Eli breathed a sigh of relief when Jacob's feet hit the ground. He watched as Jacob spoke to a few of the gathered men, probably giving them direction about what should be done directly after lunch. Then he made his way to Eli.

"Bet you don't see that in the city?" his uncle's face was red with exertion, but a smile crinkled the corners of his eyes.

Eli shook his head. "*Nee*, I bet something like this would take them weeks, months even."

"The old way is the best way." Jacob laughed as he slapped Eli on the back and headed to the drinking water.

Once the salads were all prepared, they were laid out on the trestle tables the men had set up on the lawn. Although it was only March, the sun was high in the sky and it was easily the hottest day of the year thus far. Children were playing without their coats, soaking up the lovely sunshine; they didn't even notice the slight breeze cooling them.

The tables were laden with salads, cold cuts, sandwiches and cheeses, with only the baked goods that had been placed in the kitchen yet to be put out. Joanna fell into step beside her mother as they headed to collect the sweeter treats.

"Your cake is going to cause a ruckus again," Joanna teased, bumping her mother's shoulder and causing Beatrice to laugh.

"I hope it does, it took me the better part of yesterday to prepare and bake," Beatrice said shaking her head.

Although Beatrice didn't like to flaunt her skills, she was easily the best baker in the community. Her cakes were always moist and beautifully decorated; a skill that Joanna wished she had inherited.

"I hear the bishop's wife made strudel," Joanna said, her mouth watering.

"I know. Although I have no idea how anyone

will have space for dessert. Did you see how much food there is outside?"

Joanna nodded as she opened the door for her mother to enter first. "Have you seen how much *menner* eat when they've been hard at work? There is not a doubt in my mind that not a single scrap of food will be left when they're done."

"I hope so," Beatrice smiled as she took the lid off her cake tin. "Here it is."

The rich aroma of the four layered chocolate cake drifted into the air. Joanna sighed happily. "Tell you what, let them have the food, I'll just take the cake and find a tree for myself." She lifted the cake out of the tin with a wicked smile, making her mother laugh.

"You take that cake out to the tables, young lady. All that sugar is going to cling to your hips for the rest of your life."

"Not if I don't eat anything else for the rest of the week." Joanna walked out of the kitchen with a happy smile on her face.

"Joanna, you shouldn't have," one of the men joked as she walked past him.

"I didn't, *Mamm* did," she called back.

She headed straight for the table to set the tray down for everyone to help themselves.

A few paces from the trestle table her eyes narrowed, and her heart skipped a beat. It couldn't be. She blinked a couple of times, her knees quivering from the shock as she tried to focus on his dark hair and hazel eyes.

It couldn't be…

She shook her head trying to calm her racing heart, when he turned and looked right at her. Everything disappeared. Children laughing, the conversations of men, the bark of dogs playfully yipping in the yard, even the tray that slipped from her hands and crashed to the ground.

Joanna just stood there, spellbound, staring straight ahead while Beatrice and a couple of the younger women rushed over.

"Joanna," Beatrice asked with concern when they reached her. "What happened? Are you all right?"

Joanna simply stood, unable to answer. Her gaze was fixed, disbelieving. She couldn't believe her eyes. It was him, it had to be. She would remember that smile anywhere, even after these many long and lonely years. Her breath caught as she tried to figure out how it was possible after all this time.

"Joanna," Beatrice whispered urgently. "Joanna, talk to me. What's going on?"

Joanna carefully shook her head, unable to form a single coherent sentence. She turned to look at her mother and noticed the many concerned faces surrounding her. She looked down and noticed her mother's masterpiece spilled to the ground. The chocolate cake was now nothing but a heap of icing and crumbs. She turned to her mother. "I'm so sorry… I—I uh…"

"Never mind the cake," her mother quickly assured her. "Are you alright? What happened?"

More people were gathering around her now,

wanting to see what the fuss was all about. She turned back to the object of her distraction and noticed him moving towards her. Suddenly she realized if this wasn't her mind playing tricks on her, the last thing she wanted was for him to see her standing flabbergasted over a destroyed chocolate cake.

"I'm fine, *Mamm*. I just stumbled, I'm sorry about your cake." Joanna saw the form she had been staring at start to move towards her with the rest. She couldn't allow him to see her in this state.

"Don't worry about the cake. There are plenty of tarts and pies to make do. Are you sure you're alright?"

"I'm fine. I'm just going to fetch the vanilla one," she turned and headed to the kitchen needing to get away from it all. Could you get sunstroke this early in the spring, she wondered as she rushed towards the kitchen?

She felt foolish for dropping her mother's cake but for a moment, for a few seconds, she had thought Eli Stoltzfus was back. She knew it was a foolish sentiment, probably brought on by her father's plans with Sampson King, but she needed to clear her mind of it.

Glancing over her shoulder, she couldn't help but feel guilty as her mother and a friend scooped up the ruined cake to discard of it. Luckily the Miller's had pigs, Joanna thought as she headed to the back door. At least the cake wouldn't go to waste entirely.

Her mother caught her before she stepped inside. "Joanna, are you sure you're alright? Would you like the community healer to take a look or would you like to go home?"

Joanna shook her head, forcing a smile. "I'm fine, *Mamm*, honestly. I just stumbled for a moment. I just need a minute to clear my head. I feel like such a *dummkopf*, everyone looking at me as I ruined your beautiful cake."

"Take a minute and don't worry about the cake. The vanilla one is just as *gut*," her mother assured her with a kind smile before walking back to the lunch tables.

Joanna smiled and closed the kitchen door behind her. She just needed a minute. A minute to calm her quivering senses, a moment to still her shaking hands. Joanna could feel her heart racing in her chest as she slowly drank a full glass of water and told her body to calm down. Could it really have been him after all these years? Perhaps her mind was playing tricks on her.

She was so desperate to find a way to avoid marrying Sampson, that she may very well just be seeing things. Then another thought occurred to her. Maybe this was *Gott* answering all her prayers. Over the last three days Joanna had done nothing but pray to *Gott* for a solution to the problem of a less than ideal marriage. There was no way she wanted to marry Sampson, but nor did she have the slightest desire to disobey her *daed*. She'd been praying hard for *Gott* to show her His plan. Maybe He just had.

There was also the possibility that she was slowly losing her mind and that before the week was over, she wouldn't even know who she was. A heavy sigh escaped her as she turned her back to the window and shook her head.

She took a deep breath and let it out slowly to try and slow the racing heart in her chest. She laughed silently to herself. What an idiot you are, she thought. All those hours of work wasted and all of those people thinking you are a clumsy fool because you thought you saw a ghost from the past.

She finally turned around and washed her hands.

Feeling a little steadier and a lot more foolish than before, she accepted that she couldn't hide in the kitchen forever. She took one last deep breath and decided it was time to face the music. She glanced out the window where she could already see her *daed* and *bruder* tucking into the lunch offerings with her *mamm*. Joanna watched as the men's table filled first, all of them hungry after a morning's hard work.

The children were still chasing each other while the dogs chased them; they would eat when the men were finished. She opened the other cake tin and lifted the vanilla cake out. This time, she promised herself, she wouldn't let ghosts from the past interfere with getting it to the table in one piece.

A soft laugh escaped her. What were the chances of Eli Stoltzfus showing up in Lancaster County again? She opened the door, smile still in place and her eyes widened in surprise.

Before anything was said he slipped his hands

underneath the cake tray. "Best we put this down before you drop it as well, eh?"

Her smile faltered and her eyes widened as her head slowly shook from side to side. "Eli…"

His smile broadened and her heart skipped a beat. His smile hadn't changed, but his hazel eyes no longer had the carefree look of a child. His shoulders had broadened with age and his hair seemed even blacker than she remembered.

He was wearing a T-shirt and a pair of jeans. *Englisch* clothes that seemed so out of place in the Amish setting. But beneath the *Englisch* clothes and haircut, she recognized her childhood friend. She could barely believe her eyes. Her mind clearly had not been playing tricks. *Gott* had answered her prayers.

"Joanna, I thought it was you," Eli said with a broad smile on his face. "You haven't changed a bit. Except I remember you eating cake, not dropping them." He paused for a moment before setting down the cake. "Actually, that's not strictly speaking true. You are a lot prettier than I remember."

Joanna's cheeks warmed with a blush. A frown creased her brow. Her head slowly moved from side to side.

"Joanna, are you alright? You look like you've seen a ghost. I think sheets are less pale than you are right now," his eyes were filled with humor and concern and Joanna felt the smile break through the shock as she smiled at him.

"I'm fine. I just… I didn't expect to see you again…ever!"

Eli shrugged with a grin. "Yeah, me neither."

"I didn't know that you were back!"

"I've only been here a few days, visiting…for now. I'm staying with Uncle Jacob and Aunt Delia," Eli said, pouring Joanna yet another glass of water. "I suppose word hasn't got around yet."

Joanna nodded. "*Denke*," she muttered as he handed her the glass of cold water. She took a sip, trying to process the information.

"Feel better?" he asked kindly. "I didn't mean to shock you."

He had certainly aged well, Joanna thought, looking up into his warm, welcoming eyes. "I never expected to see you again, Eli. You just disappeared one day, without a word or even a letter." There was hurt in her voice and it showed.

Eli looked crestfallen and a little ashamed. "I know," he said softly. "We left without warning. I came home from school and the cab was already waiting. You know, after the accident…"

When Eli's voice clogged with emotion, Joanna couldn't help but understand how hard leaving must have been for him.

He cleared his throat and continued. "Well, *Mamm* just couldn't cope here on her own, everything bought back memories, she said. I came home from school one day and everything was packed up. We just moved away. A clean break, she said. She wouldn't allow me to write to anyone in the community. She said it was best that way."

"Where did you end up?" Joanna asked, nodding her head at his honest reply.

"Harrisburg," replied Eli. "It was tough settling in at first. Very tough. The children at school." He stammered "Well, you can guess the reaction the Amish boy received. But over the years I started to fit in. I studied journalism."

Joanna smiled, "That sounds intriguing."

"It is. I've been a journalist at a newspaper this last year or so. I enjoy it."

"So why are you back?" Joanna asked.

Eli shrugged his shoulders. "If I'm honest, Joanna, I don't know. As far as my editor is concerned, I'm on sabbatical gathering information for stories on Amish life."

Joanna looked horrified, as though Eli was an *Englisch mann* looking to dig up dirt on their way of life and publish it for profit.

Eli laughed and raised his hand in protest, "No, that's just what I told my editor to allow me to come while keeping my job open for me. There will be no such stories. Even if I go back. The Amish deserve their respect and privacy. I might not have been home for eight years, but I still believe in our ways."

Joanna smiled. Did Eli even realize he still spoke of Lancaster as his home, or the Amish as *our* ways? Her face brightened. "I hope you enjoy your time here, Eli."

"Me too. Although I don't know how long I'll be staying yet."

Joanna immediately felt sorrow. One minute he was here, just like *Gott* had answered her prayers, the next minute he was talking about going back. "Are you going back? You aren't back here for good?"

Eli followed Joanna when she took a seat at the table. He pulled out a chair for himself and sat down with a heavy sigh. "I don't know yet. I felt a calling, something dragging me back. I think it's after *Mamm* died..."

"Your *mamm* passed? Eli, I'm so sorry to hear that." Joanna reached for his hand and squeezed it reassuringly.

"*Jah*, the cancer took her last year," he let out a sigh before summoning a smile. "So here I am. I will see what my heart tells me in a few weeks. I will see if there is a reason to stay."

Joanna was sure that Eli had looked at her in a funny way when he said that. In a way that said he wanted her to be the reason that he stayed. But she dismissed it. They had only been talking for a few minutes and they hadn't seen each other since they were children. He couldn't possibly feel the same way about her as she did about him.

Could he?

She had never forgotten him, and often lay awake at night wondering what had happened to him. Wondering if he ever thought about her.

"Joanna! Where are you?" a voice shouted from just outside the door.

"My *bruder* Jeremiah," Joanna whispered to Eli, who started to guiltily stand up. They had done nothing wrong, but it might appear strange to be found alone with Joanna in the kitchen when the whole community was picnicking outside. Eli certainly didn't want to offend anyone so soon after he had returned.

Jeremiah entered the kitchen. He looked like their father in every way. At the age of fifteen he already had their father's height and complexion.

"There you are," he said with relief in his voice. "*Mamm* was worried." He looked at Eli with suspicion in his eyes. He may have been four years younger than his sister, but he always kept a look out for her. "Who are you?" he demanded sternly.

Joanna glared at her *bruder*, annoyed by his rudeness. "This is Eli, *Bruder*. I went to school with him; you were probably too young to remember him. He had to go away when he was a *kind*. But now he is back."

A look of recognition came over Jeremiah's face. "Ah *jah*. The *Englischer*. *Daed* was just telling *Mamm* that you had come back for a while."

Joanna stood up, her face bright red, "Jeremiah. Don't use that word," she snapped. "Eli is not *Englisch*. He is Amish."

Jeremiah shrugged his shoulders as though he didn't really care either way as his eyes trailed over Eli's *Englisch* clothes and *Englisch* haircut.

Eli looked embarrassed to be the cause of the disagreement. "I probably need to go and find Jacob; he'll be wondering what has become of me." He moved towards the door. "I'm glad you are feeling a little better now, Joanna. At least the vanilla cake survived." There was a twinkle of humor in his eyes as he smiled at her. "It was a pleasure to see you again after all these years."

He nodded at Jeremiah as he walked out the door, "Nice to meet you."

Jeremiah ignored him.

"How dare you speak to one of my friends like that?" Joanna demanded once Eli had walked out of earshot.

"One of your friends, is he? You don't know him. And I'm sure *Daed* won't be pleased about you being friends with an *Englischer*."

"He's not *Englisch*, I keep telling you. Eli is Amish."

"He's wearing *Englisch* clothes, speaks with an *Englisch* accent...walk like a duck, talk like a duck? Besides, everyone here would think of him as *Englisch*," Jeremiah insisted.

"Well, I don't care for your opinion, little *bruder*," Joanna said sharply, with a face that would curdle milk. "He is my friend and you will not be so rude next time you see him. Understand?"

"Fine," he said holding up his hands in mock surrender. "We had better go outside; *Mamm* will come looking for us and that cake in a minute."

They left to join the others, Joanna still fuming with anger. But also, a little confused.

Eli probably really was *Englisch* now.

A dozen thoughts sprung to mind at once as she helped herself to the potato salad on offer. Why was Eli back? Did he perhaps feel the same strong connection she had felt when she had looked into his eyes?

Was it possible to fall in love with someone you had not seen for eight years in just a few minutes? A grin tugged at the corners of her mouth as she spotted him serving himself a slice of her *mamm*'s vanilla cake with a crooked smile aimed at her.

Butterflies zapped through her tummy, but she couldn't seem to look away. She couldn't help but feel hopeful about her future for the first time in months. When Eli had left, they had been no more than childhood friends, but the way he looked at her today made her wonder if there could possibly be more than friendship.

He was no longer Amish; he had never even been baptized, but she couldn't help but wonder if he might stay. If he did, would he court her? The thoughts kept coming, strange and unexpected and all too exciting. They were all too soon interrupted by her mother.

"Joanna, I see the vanilla cake made it safely to the table?"

"*Jah*. Luckily it did," Joanna smiled at her mother.

"Did you see Eli is back?"

"Jah, she did. They were talking in the kitchen.

I don't much like him," Jeremiah said, judgment clear in his voice.

Her father cleared his throat and wiped his mouth with a napkin before saying his piece. "It is not our place to judge, Jeremiah. Eli Stoltzfus lost his father at a young age and his mother barely a year ago. I think in a certain way Lancaster County is the last place he remembers having his whole *familye* together. I think while he is visiting, we should welcome him and make him feel like one of us."

"While he's wearing *Englisch* clothes?" Jeremiah asked, confused.

"A man's clothing is not of importance. It's what's in his heart that matters," Beatrice said softly with a smile for Joanna.

Joanna felt hope bloom in her chest. Perhaps her father was right. Perhaps Eli was searching for the happiness he had left behind in Lancaster County, and perhaps she could show him that he could have that happiness here once again.

Chapter Five

The Box

For more than a week Joanna didn't see Eli again. Although that didn't mean out of sight, out of mind. She thought of him most of the day and couldn't help but wonder if he was enjoying his time in Lancaster County.

For so long she hadn't thought of him at all and now it seemed she couldn't stop. She wanted to know what it was like in the city. Did he have friends? Did he have a girlfriend? Why was he here?

But most importantly she wondered if he would stay.

On church Sunday, the service was held in the Miller's new barn. Joanna had sat on the left side with the other women and daughters, the men on the right. She spotted him sitting in the back and noticed, even though he wasn't in plain clothes, he had worn a white shirt and black trousers out of re-spect for the community.

The sermon could have been written just for her, Joanna thought as she listened. The bishop spoke about second chances, forgiveness, and taking *Gott*'s hand when you needed direction in your life. Was that why Eli was here? When the service was over, she couldn't help but hope for a moment with him, but they shared nothing but a smile before her father summoned them to the buggy to return home. Usu-ally they would stay for the traditional community luncheon after the service, but her father wanted to get home to tend to an ill horse. Joanna left with a heavy heart, knowing however that she would see him again.

It was as if somewhere in her heart *Gott* was telling her that Eli came back for a reason, and she couldn't help but believe that reason involved her. It was a foolish notion, she knew, but one that strengthened with every passing day.

By Monday Joanna knew she wouldn't see Eli if she didn't make some kind of effort. Since it would be inappropriate for her to call on the Stoltzfus farm just to see him, she came up with another plan. She explained to her mother that she wanted to get a little more exercise after putting on some weight over the winter. Her mother, having always been conscious of her own weight, eagerly agreed that she shed the extra pounds now before it refused to budge like hers.

The first morning Joanna had walked past the

Stoltzfus farm, her eyes peeled for Eli, but she didn't see him even briefly. The second day she caught sight of him walking into the woods at the edge of the farm with a shovel over his shoulder. Curiosity tugged at her, but she kept walking in the direction of her home.

The third time she again saw Eli head into the woods, again with the shovel, and she couldn't help but wonder if he was lying about his true reason for coming to visit his aunt and uncle. What could be in the woods that Eli didn't want anyone to know about?

The fourth, or fifth time, she couldn't be sure, she decided to follow him. But by the time she'd made up the distance, he had disappeared into the thick copse of trees, and she couldn't follow him to see what he was up to.

It all seemed very suspicious. She couldn't think of a single job or task that would need doing in the woods that would involve digging. Especially since Jacob was a carpenter, why would he have Eli digging in the woods? Her mind filled with a thousand terrible thoughts. She tried to dismiss them. Eli had been so kind when she had had spoken to him the other day, surely there was no suspicious or ulterior motive to him being here.

On the positive side, Sampson King was still fighting the flu, so she been spared further talk of a possible marriage, and the dinner with the Kings had been postponed until further notice. It seemed a long bout of flu to Joanna. She'd had it the previous winter and although it was severe enough to see her confined to her sick bed, she had only been down for three days. Joanna couldn't help but be concerned. Although she and Sampson had never been friends, she wished him no ill, especially not with a prolonged flu.

She felt guilty for feeling relief that her parents' plan to match her had been interfered with, but this too shall pass, she knew. As soon as Sampson was back on his feet, her parents would insist on the dinner with the King *familye*.

She felt even more guilty for thinking about Eli most of the time. Her mind constantly drifted back to the times when they were children and how she and Eli would play in the stream in the woods, kicking water over each other so they would return to their houses soaking wet. Joanna often got scolded by her *mamm* for dirtying her clothing, but she had never minded. She and Eli had such fun together.

Two weeks since the barn raising and the fateful reunion with Eli, Joanna was alone in the house when she heard the familiar clip-clop of horse hooves. A frown creased her brow knowing that she wasn't expecting company. Her father and brother were sowing the west field this morning and weren't expected back until lunch time. Her mother had gone into town to do some shopping and to deliver a cake to the bishop's wife. She pulled back the curtain and glanced outside, surprised to see their grey gelding, Harry, running free in the direction of the dirt road.

Knowing this could only end in disaster, Joanna

dropped what she was doing and rushed after him. One glance at the gate that led to Harry's field explained everything. Harry was a clever horse and easily maneuvered a gate to open if it wasn't secured properly. The gate swung in the wind, the rope that should have been used to secure it was hanging over the railing.

This wasn't the first time Jeremiah had forgotten to secure the gate. Joanna shook her head and started running. She had about two miles of dirt road before Harry would rush into traffic. Two miles to catch him and entice him back home.

The last time it had taken her dad and Jeremiah almost two hours to secure the horse. Harry was obedient but when faced with freedom, he might as well be a wild horse.

She ran out into the road calling after the horse, but he paid no attention and continued happily on his way. Instead of rushing straight ahead to the main road, Harry cut across a field through another open gate.

What was it with this community and leaving gates open, Joanna wondered as she began to feel her lungs burn? She chased him over the field, past Jacob's farm in the distance and into the woodland beyond.

Joanna buckled down and rushed ahead. Instead of the balmy spring mornings they had been blessed with over the last few weeks, today was a cold morning. The drizzle wouldn't stop, making her chase even harder. Concern washed over her as she realized that Harry was running full speed into a wooded area that was strange to him.

He'll break his neck, Joanna feared, and tried to run quicker. As she rushed into the woods, she realized the early morning fog was yet to lift here. She could barely see a few paces ahead of her; the only sound was her labored breathing.

The woods where she had played as a child suddenly seemed creepy and more than a little intimidating. She ran deeper into the undergrowth, calling Harry's name louder and louder.

"Harry!" Joanna slowed her pace, afraid she would fall and break something before she found the wayward horse. "Harry please! I promise I'll give you carrots; you can even pluck some beetroot out of the vegetable garden. Please, just come back!"

Joanna searched and called for what felt like hours until she realized she was completely lost in the woods. She stopped and turned around, recognizing she had no idea of direction. She tried to catch her breath, listening for any sound of Harry when suddenly a twig snapped behind her and she spun around praying for it to be Harry. But she could see nothing in the misty gloom. Fear gripped at her throat, making her knees tremble as she kept moving further into the thick wooded area.

She pressed further forward, wishing she'd brought a lantern with her. She emerged from the dark trees into a small, well-lit clearing. A few sun beams managed to fight through the canopy of trees and light up the area where the fog had cleared.

In the center of the clearing was Harry. Out of breath and clearly as fit as a fiddle. But he was not alone. He stood for a man to stroke his nose. Joanna frowned as the man stepped around the horse and then joy filled her heart.

"Eli?"

"Joanna?" he exclaimed. "Is this your horse? I found him wandering, lost in the woods."

"Harry," said a very relieved Joanna, rushing forward and throwing her arms around the horse's neck. "I'm so glad you found him, Eli. He managed to escape our field; I don't think the gate was closed properly. I've been chasing him for hours."

"He's a fine-looking gelding," praised Eli, stroking his flank. "I'm just glad I was here. He could easily have broken his leg walking around here in the gloom."

Joanna sighed, relieved, "I know." When she finally caught her breath, a frown creased her brow as she noticed a series of small holes dug in the clearing. All were about three feet deep. She turned slowly and noticed the shovel lying to one side.

So, this was what Eli was doing in the woods? But why numerous three-foot holes? Confusion mingled with fear as she turned back to Eli. Something inched down her spine, reminding her that she no longer knew Eli now that the years had marched on since their childhood friendship. A lot could change in eight years. He could have become...

She quickly pushed the thought away as she stepped carefully towards Harry. "I'll take him from here." She avoided meeting Eli's gaze, unsure of what she had stumbled across.

Eli frowned at her before he began chuckling. "Don't worry; it's not what it looks like. Besides, what could I possibly bury in a three-foot-deep hole?"

Joanna shrugged, still not satisfied with his explanation. "I think it's better if Harry and I just leave. *Denke* for your help."

"Joanna, no wait. I can explain, honestly."

"I don't know if I want to hear an explanation," Joanna said, a little uncertainly.

Eli began making a noose with the length of rope he pulled from his bag. He gently slipped it over Harry's neck and tied the other end around a sturdy old tree. He pulled it tight, making sure it was secure.

"There," he said with a satisfied smile. "This fine fellow is going nowhere on his own now. Catch your breath and I'll explain." He paused and looked around at the strange series of holes, shaking his head before a smile tugged at the corners of his mouth. "What was I doing?" He took a deep breath. "This is going to be harder than I thought, Joanna."

"I'm sorry," Joanna blurted out "I didn't mean to pry. It is just that I've seen you a few times over this last week heading into the woods with that shovel." She pointed to the shovel that was still stuck in the ground, protruding from one of the questionable holes. "No one tends to do that around here that much."

Eli glanced around the clearing; the sweat was glistening on his brow from the exertion of all his digging despite the coolness of the misty morning. He laughed at the scene unfolding before him. "I guess this all looks kind of odd."

Joanna nodded nervously, "To be honest, it does. You show up out of nowhere after eight years with a story of a sabbatical. And each day I see you heading out here, shovel over your shoulder. Do Jacob and Delia know what you're up to? Would the bishop have granted you permission to come if he knew?" She pointed to the nearest hole. "You've obviously come here to dig for something."

Eli went down on his haunches and then slumped to the ground. He wiped his damp hair out of his eyes and grabbed the bottle of water he had brought with him, taking a deep drink. He waved at a fallen tree next to him.

"Do you wanna sit down? This is a story that will take a little time in the telling."

Joanna glanced at Harry who was happily chomping down on a patch of grass at his feet and made a split-second decision. Joanna wasn't sure if she wanted to hear the story. She could take the horse and walk away and spend the rest of her life wondering. Or she could stay and listen and possibly become the victim to be chopped up and buried bit by bit in his three-foot holes.

But inquisitiveness got the better of her, so she perched on the log next to him.

"Do you remember how my *daed* died?" Eli asked.

Joanna searched the remnants of her brain for the answer, "It was some kind of accident, if I recall correctly. But I couldn't tell you exactly."

"He fell off a barn roof that he was repairing over at the King's farm."

The King's farm.

Everything seemed to revolve around the Kings at the moment. If only Eli knew what her *daed* had planned, Joanna thought, but she decided to keep this vital piece of information to herself for the present moment.

"That morning at breakfast he was just his normal, jovial self. I didn't know he would leave for work and never come back to us again. If I'd known, there would have been more I had to say to him, more I would have asked. You just don't believe that something like that can happen."

A stray tear coursed across his face. Joanna wasn't used to seeing men cry and didn't know how to react. She immediately felt as if she wanted to comfort the vulnerable young man, but at the same time she didn't feel it appropriate, especially considering she wasn't yet sure if she might be destined to be his victim.

He managed to control his emotions and continued his story. "Then I came home from school and the *haus* was awash with people. Can you imagine how terrible it was learning that your *daed* was dead in the face of half the community?"

Joanna shook her head. *That must have been truly awful*, she thought. And she in turn battled to fight back the tears thinking of her young friend so obviously distraught.

"*Mamm* was a wreck after the funeral. Until he was buried, the community was always around the *haus*. The bishop came, the widows' group; everyone offering food and all manner of help. And then immediately after the funeral there was a period of silence during which we were left alone. It was the worst thing that could possibly have happened to my *mamm*. One moment we had everyone's support and the next we were left to continue our lives in peace, but without my father. She was left alone to grieve and to be alone with her thoughts. What she really needed was to be around people. I never saw her sleep in the weeks following his death; she was always nervously fretting, playing with her hands over and over again. She never raised a word in anger to me. But I could tell that in her heart she was full of resentment."

"Eli, I'm so sorry; it must have been a terrible time for both of you. I can't imagine…"

Eli nodded, "I was angry, Joanna. Not angry at my *mamm*, I can understand how upset she must have been; still a young woman in her late thirties with a *kind* to look after. No, I wasn't angry at my *mamm*, I was angry at my *daed*. Angry that he hadn't been more careful on the roof. I was angry at the Kings, employing him to do the job. I was angry at *Gott* and the rain He had sent that morning to make the roof slippery. I was angry at everyone and everything. And there were always those reminders of my *daed* around me. You're right; it was hard."

Joanna didn't know why but she brushed a hand over his back in a quiet show of support.

"Before we buried him, my *mamm* took me to view him in the coffin," Eli paused and shook his head as though he couldn't quite believe the story he was telling. "I can still see his coffin lying in our *haus*, and all the people coming to pay their respects. She took two locks of his hair, one for her, one for me."

He took another drink and caught his breath. His voice had started cracking with the emotion of the telling, and he took a few moments to collect himself.

"One night I woke up to my mother's crying. I didn't know how to make it better for her. I was now the *mann* of the *haus* and there was nothing I could do to console her. The anger rushed over me like a red fog. I grabbed a little box my father had made for me for me when I was young and began putting every memory of him inside it."

Joanna frowned, "Like a memory box?"

"No, this wasn't for memories, this was to forget," Eli sighed. "I was young, angry and distraught. Thinking back now, a memory box would have been a better idea. Anyway, I put in the letters he had written me when I was in hospital with my broken leg, the lock of hair my mother had given me, and my *daed*'s bible. In the front were the inscriptions of our entire *familye*'s births and deaths. It was a sacred piece of our heritage, but I didn't care at the time. I just wanted the reminders of him out of my life so that my mother could finally move on."

"What did you do with the box?" Joanna asked, shaking her head when suddenly it dawned on her. A ghost of smile played on her mouth. "You buried it out here, didn't you?"

Eli nodded, "I snuck out the back of the *haus* without my *mamm* even realizing I had left. If she had come up to my bedroom, she would have been mortified. I grabbed a shovel from the shed and ran into the woods with nothing but a lantern to guide the way. As I ran, the anger grew while the tears streamed down my face. I reached a little clearing, and just on its edge I dug a hole and buried the box. Maybe I was trying to bury my anger and hurt with those memories. I soon came to regret my actions. You see, the very next day I arrived home from school and *Mamm* had already packed all our stuff. Within ten minutes of me walking through the door, we were leaving the community for good." He rubbed at his eyes which were shining with tears.

Joanna held her tongue, giving him a moment to compose himself, "And you left all the memories of your father behind."

Sadness overwhelmed her even as the realization dawned on her that Eli wasn't back because of her. He was only back to find the memories of his father he had buried so long ago.

"It didn't take me long to regret burying that

box. It was all I had to remember him by. It has been slowly eating me up, year after year. I really hoped when I came back here that I would find it. Do you know how many clearings there are in these woods?"

Joanna shook her head at the question.

"Hundreds. The stupid thing is that I have no idea which clearing I ended up in that night. I have been digging every day for the past week. Nothing."

"That's terrible," said Joanna, wiping her own tears away with her hand. She hadn't even realized she had started crying until she tasted a tear on her lips. She wasn't even sure why she was crying. Because Eli hadn't come back because of her or because Eli had lost his father and now couldn't even find the memories he should have cherished?

Eli laughed wryly. "You know what the worst part is? I can't even blame anyone for my stupidity. I should never have buried that box. Why didn't I just put it at the bottom of my closet, or under my bed like a normal person would have done?"

"I can't believe what you must have been through. You were grieving, Eli, it's hard to understand the decision someone makes when they've suffered a loss. You'll find it."

She felt inexplicably guilty hearing Eli bare his soul to her. She remembered her own feelings when she heard that he had left the community without even saying goodbye. Nobody tells a child the real circumstances, do they? She had in her mind all these years that it was Eli's decision to leave, but of course at that age there was no way it could be. She had been angry at him for no reason.

"It has been difficult since I came back. I hoped I would get some kind of message, perhaps *Gott* would talk to me. I wanted peace. Resolution. I hoped that finding my box would help me find that resolution. But to be honest, I don't know why *Gott* would talk to me. I've never heard Him before. It would probably be best if I just leave the past buried where it should be. Perhaps I should go back to where I belong now."

He started to raise his voice as his anger grew inside him. He stood up and glanced around himself. "What are the chances of finding a clearing I happened upon in the middle of the night more than eight years ago? Who was I fooling?"

Joanna's heart sank. Just a few days ago he was full of talk of staying in the community for good. There was no real suggestion of simply having returned to give it a try. Although that was the way she had played the conversation in her own head, in fact she'd leapt ahead and seen him baptized, then taking buggy rides together, followed by an engagement. Now, the second time they spoke, he was speaking of returning to his *Englisch* world and leaving her again. All those crazy ideas that had been leaping around in her head started to disappear, one by one.

Joanna watched Eli and felt her heart clench in her chest. She had loved the boy and was slowly falling in love with the *mann*, but it seemed that he was already planning on leaving again. She wanted to jump up and tell him that Lancaster County was his home, but knew it wasn't her place. The connection she had shared with Eli all those years ago was still there for her, but who was to say it was still there for him? Had he really been her friend, or had he simply taken pity on a little girl?

Tears burned the back of her eyes at the thought. She couldn't stand the idea of losing him again, but then it wasn't her decision. The decision was Eli's.

She thought of all the hardships he had faced in his life already, losing both parents and now the memories of his father, and knew that possibly *Gott* had brought him back into her life for another reason. Perhaps Joanna should try and be the friend he so desperately needed when it felt like he was all alone in the world. Maybe if she was the friend he needed, he would come to realize that this was where he belonged. Joanna already knew she would pray for more, but for now she was simply a tool in *Gott*'s plan for Eli.

"Listen, don't rush into a decision," Joanna said. "You have three months, you told me at the barn raising. Use those months to put your mother and father's memories to rest, Eli. I know you miss him, but you need to move on with your own life."

Eli spun around, anger flashing in his eyes. "Don't you think I've tried that? That's why I finally ended up here. It's like I can't find happiness. I remember how happy we were as *kinners*. For some reason I expected it to be that way when I came back. It isn't."

Joanna sighed, shaking her head. "It is a big leap from the outside world. You haven't lived a plain life in years; give yourself some time to adjust. Give yourself three months."

Trying to lighten the heavy atmosphere filled with pain and sorrow, she tried to make a joke, "There is a lot of digging that you can do in that period of time. Especially if there is an extra pair of hands ready to help."

Eli frowned for a moment before he understood. "Joanna, I couldn't ask you to help me," he looked sheepish. "Digging isn't any work for woman."

"Really? And where did you come up with that notion? In Harrisburg? I'll have you know that here in Amish country it's the women who plant the kitchen gardens. Every vegetable you eat was planted by a woman. As for me… I'm quite an accomplished gardener. I have quite a way with a shovel, *denke*," she laughed, trying to put him at his ease.

"Well, I'd certainly appreciate an extra pair of hands now and then," Eli conceded with a grin. "It would help if I knew where to start." He sighed and dragged a hand through his hair before smiling at her sheepishly.

Joanna's stomach flipped at Eli's warm smile. And she suddenly realized she would be spending a lot more time with him over the coming weeks. She couldn't help but be excited at the prospect.

"I'll give it the full three months. See what happens. At this point, I simply don't know," Eli said with a serious face. He held her gaze. "Spiritual fulfillment and a simple life are all well and good. But obviously I hope there might be other benefits as well."

"Like what?" Joanna laughed. "Home cooked meals and organic vegetables?"

"*Nee*," Eli said, sobering. "The company of an old friend."

Joanna's stomach flipped yet again. If she interpreted his words correctly, she was the other benefit. She decided that they had better get home. Her mind was playing funny tricks on her. Here, alone in the woods with Eli, she did not want to be tempted. Besides, her *familye* might be back and wondering where she had gone off to, all alone with Harry the horse.

"Right," she declared. "That is sorted then. You'll stay; I'll help dig when I can. And now you can walk me home. Actually, you can walk Harry home. I'll take the shovel." She smiled over her shoulder as she began her walk further into the woods when Eli cleared his throat.

"Joanna! You live the other way."

"Right," Joanna turned around with a frown, realizing she was completely and utterly lost.

Eli expertly guided the horse out of the woods without causing his footing to falter. Out on the fields the passage became a lot easier. As they walked, they fell into an easy pace.

"So, did you enjoy it in Harrisburg?" Joanna had promised herself she wouldn't pry, but how could she not? There was a whole eight years of Eli's life she knew nothing about.

Eli shrugged, still holding the lead on Harry, "At first it was intimidating. I didn't know anything the other kids did. They went to movies, had cell phones, watched television shows I had never heard about… It took time, but finally I made friends and it became easier."

"I can't imagine having to leave everything I know. And your *mamm*?"

Eli chuckled quietly, "I don't know if it was because she was trying to forget my father or if she truly enjoyed it, but she took to being *Englisch* like a duck to water. Looking back now, I think that helped a great deal with the grief."

Joanna nodded. She couldn't imagine burying the happy times only to force yourself into a new life. "And your friends? Do they know you're here?"

Eli nodded, "Friends in the city aren't like friends in the community. I have a few friends, but everyone is so caught up in their own lives, their careers and their own futures, we're lucky to catch up every couple of weeks. I told one I was coming back. You know what he told me?"

"What?" Joanna asked truly intrigued.

"He asked me why I waited so long. He said that I always had a sad look in my eyes and hopefully coming here would be what was needed to take it away. He went on to tell me that I could focus on my career when I got back, but I ignored that part."

"Are careers really so important in the city?"

Joanna asked, dumbfounded. In Lancaster County *familye* and faith were by far the most important. Sure, everyone had talent and skill, and they used it to provide for their *familye*, but not to chase achievement.

"You wouldn't believe it. When I was in high school," Eli laughed at Joanna's surprised look. "Yeah, my aunt insisted if I was going to be *Englisch*, I needed high school. Anyway, even in the eighth grade they start planning their careers. It's all about where you work, what you earn and what belongings you have as testimony to your wealth. I must admit, for a while there I managed to look past that but being back here just made me realize how focused they are on wealth."

"How is it going with Uncle Jacob and Aunt Delia? Are they glad to have you back?"

Eli laughed, "If it were up to them, I'd be tied down in the barn to stop me from leaving. Delia has procured a set of plain clothes for me. Told me the other night I should have a pair when the time came to start wearing them again."

"When will that be?"

Eli shrugged with a sigh, "I don't know, Joanna. Right now, I don't know who I am or where I want to be. I just don't think it is right to start wearing plain clothes if I haven't figured that out yet. I'll just be giving the bishop and my *familye* the impression that I am staying when I haven't decided yet. I have a life in the city. I have an apartment, a job…and now I sound just like those people I told you about."

Joanna laughed, "*Jah*, you do. Did you court in the city?"

Eli held her gaze for a moment before a smile played on his mouth. "We don't court in the city, we date. And there have been a few girls but none that I would call girlfriend material. How about you, miss nosy cheeks, are you being courted? I bet the men are begging for you ride with them at singings."

Joanna quickly shook her head as a blush colored her cheeks. "None that I would call husband material," she replied a little more cheekily than usual. "So, what did you do when you weren't working?"

"I used to go horse riding in the beginning. *Mamm* paid for riding lessons but it didn't stick for long. We couldn't afford it." He tenderly brushed a hand over the horse's flank and smiled at her. "But Uncle Jacob insisted I learn my way around horses again. Said he isn't driving me anywhere."

"I was wondering why you were so good with Henry. He's usually a little skittish around strange people."

"Maybe I'm only strange to you, but we'll remedy that during our digging excursions."

Joanna laughed, shaking her head. "*Jah*, I'm sure we will, stranger."

As they approached Joanna's *haus*, they saw her *mamm*, *daed* and *bruder* out on the porch. Joanna's *daed* raced down the road towards them.

"Joanna, where on earth have you been?" he demanded angrily, glaring at Eli. "You've made your *mamm* sick with worry."

"*Daed*, Harry escaped from the field. Jeremiah must have failed to secure the gate last night. I had to chase him down the road. He ran over the fields and then into the woods. We were lucky. Eli was in the woods and he managed to catch Harry for us."

Her father turned around to cast a furious glance at Jeremiah before turning back to Joanna. "I'm just glad you got him."

"Like I said, it's all Eli. He managed to catch Harry and he has walked us both home. I'd never have been able to do all that on my own. The gelding was having the time of his life, still would be if it hadn't been for Eli."

Her *daed* gave her a look that suggested he didn't believe her. But he was also aware that his daughter did not tell lies.

"*Denke*," he muttered to Eli. "Harry is like *familye*, we would have hated for anything to have happened to him. *Denke* for bringing him and my *dochder* home."

"My pleasure," said Eli warmly, trying to force a smile from Joanna's *daed*. He didn't succeed.

"Right, come on. Let's get you inside," her *daed* said to Joanna. "I'll take Harry to the field. You'd better go in and make your *mamm* a cup of tea. Calm her nerves. When she came back from town to find the *haus* and the field deserted, all manner of thoughts fried her brain."

He took the rope out of Eli's hand with an acknowledging nod. With his free hand he grasped his daughter's arm and pulled her away.

Joanna turned and said, "Thank you, Eli."

She couldn't understand why her father was acting so strangely as she released herself from his
grip. "I thought you'd be happy that Henry was returned home safely."

As soon as they were out of earshot, her *daed*
whispered to Joanna, "I don't want you see too much
of that *Englischer*."

"But, *Daed*," Joanna protested, "Eli is not an
Englischer. He is Amish just like you and me. He
was forced to leave, you know he didn't do it by
choice, and it was his choice to return. You can't
be suggesting the bishop turned him away to have
him shunned?"

"Of course, we aren't going to shun him or turn
him away," replied her *daed*, crossly. "We can't shun
him. Because he isn't Amish!"

"He is," Joanna insisted. It was the first time
she had argued with her father and knew he wasn't
happy about it. But she couldn't believe her father
would be so obtuse about a man who had only tried
to help. "I'm going to make *Mamm* some tea." She
sighed heavily as she walked back to the house shaking her head.

In the distance she saw Eli walking back to his
uncle's farm and felt horrible for the way her father
had treated him.

Joanna walked into the kitchen and found her
mother sitting at the table, her face pale with worry.
"I'm sorry, *Mamm*, I should have left a note or something, but Harry was running so fast…"

"It's alright, my *dochder*. I just didn't know what had become of you. I'm glad Eli was there to help."

"Me too." Joanna began making her mother a cup of tea and couldn't help but wonder if she would see Eli again. She had promised to help him search for the buried chest, but after her father's insistent demand that she not see him again, she couldn't imagine going against her father's wishes.

Knowing the answers weren't in her mind, she closed her eyes as she waited for the water to boil, and she prayed.

Gott, please help me understand why You brought Eli back into my life. Please make it clear to me what You expect of me. I want to be his friend, to help him find his happiness again but I don't want to disrespect my daed. Help me, Gott, show me the way. Amen.

Chapter Six

Digging for the Past

Since her father had told her he didn't want her to see Eli, not another word was mentioned on the subject. It had been almost a week since he had saved Harry in the woods and Joanna couldn't help but wonder if he had found the buried box yet.

She remembered her promise to help him search for it, a promise she couldn't make good on until now because she had been under her father's careful watch. A few times she thought about asking her mother to talk to her father about it but decided against it. Her mother wasn't very predictable with matters such as these. On the one hand she might agree that Joanna should be permitted to spend time with her childhood friend. On the other, she might tell Joanna to never ask again. It was because of the possibility of the latter that Joanna avoided the subject at all cost.

Not even Jeremiah, who was usually a chatter-box about everything happening in the community, mentioned Eli Stoltzfus's name again.

On Friday morning after the morning chores were done, her father announced that it was time to go to town. Usually when her brother and her father headed to town together, it could take the whole day. She and her mother usually tagged along to peek into the stores in town and maybe purchase fabric, thread or ingredients needed to make preserves and cake.

Normally it was a town day for the entire Lapp *familye*. But not today. When the sun had kissed her eyelids early that morning summoning her to rise, a pounding headache came with wakefulness. Even after her mother had made her get back into bed with a hot cup of medicinal chamomile tea, the headache persisted.

"I think it's best you stay home today, Joanna. You'll only feel worse if you go into town," her mother urged, handing Joanna two pills. Although the Amish preferred natural remedies, there were times that called for a stronger relief.

"You're right. I think I'm going to draw the drapes and stay in bed until this headache clears."

"I hope you're not coming down with the fever," Beatrice said, concern shining in her eyes. "You know that Sampson still hasn't recovered from the flu. It's a bad one too, I hear."

Joanna swallowed, trying to assess whether she had any symptoms besides the headache. "*Nee*, I think it's just a headache. I'm sure I'll be fine if I sleep a little."

"*Gut*, I'll leave a pot of tea on the stove for when you wake up. Make sure to eat, Joanna."

"I will, *Mamm. Denke*, and enjoy your day," Joanna rolled over after she swallowed the tablets, and closed her eyes. She couldn't help but wonder if the headache wasn't the result of her worrying over the last couple of days.

She was worried about Sampson not getting better, not because she liked him but because she cared like any other person would. She was concerned about Eli not finding the box and returning to his *Englisch* life without having the answers he wanted. She was worried…

A heavy sigh escaped her as she remembered the verse from the bible her mother always repeated.

Philippians 4: 6-7: Do not be anxious about anything, but in everything by prayer and supplication with thanksgiving, let your requests be made known to God.

A warm calmness settled over her as her eyes drifted close. She cast her worries onto *Gott*, and soon sleep dragged her under.

When she woke up, she tentatively opened her eyes hoping the headache had abated. When she realized the throbbing behind her eyes was gone, she sighed and climbed out of bed. It was shortly before lunch, she realized as she pulled back the drapes and glanced at the sun's location.

After a cup of tea and a slice of toast, she wondered what to do with the rest of the afternoon. Her family wouldn't be back until dinner time and all the chores had been taken care of. It was a whimsical thought, but she decided to do it anyway. After cleaning the kitchen and getting dressed, Joanna stepped out into the warm spring afternoon. The fresh air kissed her cheeks as if *Gott*'s grace itself was making itself known.

With a smile on her face, she headed out for an easy stroll. Just because she was walking in the direction of the Stoltzfus farm didn't mean she was going to see Eli…

But she couldn't help but hope that she would.

She walked at a leisurely pace, enjoying the balmy afternoon. Twice she stopped to look at a flower or a butterfly playing on the petals of a fresh bloom. By the time she walked past Jacob Stoltzfus's fields, she felt much better than she had that morning. She was pleasantly surprised to find Eli out in the yard chopping wood. He looked very handsome and strong as he worked up a sweat in the late-morning spring air.

For a moment she considered going back home. Wouldn't it be obvious for her to show up here? She didn't have a chance to change her mind when Eli called out to her.

"Joanna!" he smiled as he waved at her from a distance. "You just made the day even more perfect than it already was."

A blush colored her cheeks as she returned the smile. She couldn't just turn around and walk back now. She had to at least say hello. She crossed the field, stepping carefully. The last thing she wanted was to fall flat on her face with Eli as witness.

"Hullo, Eli," Joanna replied when she joined him.

"What's a pretty girl like you doing walking alone on a beautiful day such as today?" Eli's smile made the corners of his eyes wrinkle. She had never thought age could suit a man, but the eight years he had been away suited Eli handsomely.

"*Ach*, my whole *familye* is in town. I woke up with a headache and stayed behind. When I woke this afternoon, I thought the fresh air would do me good."

"It did, your cheeks are rosy with a healthy glow."

Joanna forced a smile—he didn't know her cheeks were rosy for another reason. "Have you found the box yet?"

Eli shook his head as he set the axe against the wall. "*Nee*. I've dug and dug and come up with nothing but dirt." He chuckled at his own joke. "I was thinking of heading there a little later."

"Would you like some company?" Joanna had not planned on spending the afternoon with Eli but suddenly knew there was no better way for her to spend her day.

Eli's face brightened at the suggestion. "Sure. Let me just put the axe away and grab some shovels."

Joanna laughed, "Anyone not knowing what we're doing might think we're going into the woods to bury a body."

Eli shrugged, but a sad smile spread across his face. "Or bury the questions I can't seem to answer."

Joanna nodded, "You'll find the answers, Eli, just look to *Gott* and not to yourself."

"I know," a frown creased his brow. "Joanna, I can't help but think that your *daed* doesn't approve of me. I don't want your helping me to cause trouble for you with your *familye*?"

Joanna knew her father didn't approve; she also knew that this was her opportunity to agree and walk away, but her feet wouldn't move. Something inside her told her that even though her father didn't approve, what she was doing wasn't wrong...

"I'd like to apologize for his rudeness, he did not mean anything by it. He was simply worried because I had seemingly gone missing. He doesn't normally behave the way he did," Joanna said, not mentioning the conversation that had immediately followed regarding not spending too much time with the *Englischer*.

"Okay then. If you are sure. I certainly don't want to get you into any trouble by spending time with me. Digging in the woods is probably not considered appropriate activity for a young woman like you."

Joanna shook her head. "It will be fine, so unless you want to waste more time talking about it, let's go," she insisted, making sure that was clear in Eli's mind.

She knew that the *Englisch* had a different idea of what was proper and what was improper. Eli had spent his teenage years with the *Englisch*, so she thought she would make sure he knew the boundaries. "Besides, we will be digging…and hopefully finding your buried treasure."

Eli nodded his agreement, grabbed two shovels from the shed and balanced them on his broad shoulders. "Okay then. Let's go digging."

As they entered the thick wooded area, Joanna couldn't help but glance around with more than just a little concern.

"Eli, not to be a wet blanket, but do you have any idea where you buried the box? These woods are quite thick; we might dig for years and not find it."

Eli shrugged, "Honestly, I have no idea. Despite the full moon on the night I buried it, all I remember was rushing into the woods until I came across the clearing. I didn't even put a rock or something on top of it to mark the spot. *Ferhoodled* of me, right?"

Joanna smiled at his use of the word *ferhoodled*. It warmed her heart to know that even having spent so much of his time in the *Englisch* world, he hadn't forgotten their favorite word.

"I think it's *ferhoodled* of you to think you're going to find it," she teased back.

Joanna thought to herself as they walked how over the years those clearings could have changed shape, become smaller as the trees encroached, or become bigger as some of the vegetation died away, especially after the droughts of recent years. Was there any chance of finding the box after all these years? She doubted it. Even if they did find it, there was no certainty the contents inside would be undamaged; damp had a devastating effect on paper.

But while they searched, there was hope. And there was *Gott*.

They walked into a tiny clearing and Joanna said enthusiastically, "Where shall we start?"

"Not this one," Eli replied, pointing to a piece of white ribbon tied around one of the thinner trees on the edge of the clearing. "I've already searched here. I leave those pieces of ribbon as markers. One clearing looks much like another. Even when you're a grown *mann* with a good sense of direction."

"Very clever," agreed Joanna and they pressed on deeper into the woods.

They navigated their way through the thick underbrush and large trees just budding with new life after a long cold winter. In their own way the trees resembled her feelings for Eli. For such a long time she hadn't thought of him, and now her feelings for him were blooming again.

"So..." Joanna said after a while as she stepped over a tree root. "Tell me about Harrisburg."

Eli sighed with smile. "What do you want to know? There's so much I can tell you. I can tell you about how *gut* high school was; I can tell you about going to the movies and watching a film on a wall the size of the barn..."

Joanna laughed, "*Nee*! It can't be. Who would want a television that big?"

Eli didn't chasten her for not understanding, instead he explained patiently as they walked.

When he was finished, Joanna turned to him with

a curious frown. "Did you take any girls to these barn-sized theatres?"

Curiosity was clear in her voice after he mentioned that taking a girl to the movies was a common occurrence in the *Englisch* world.

"*Nee*. But a few did catch a lift with me in my car."

Joanna laughed, "You can drive a car."

"I had to," Eli shrugged. "It's the only way to get around Harrisburg conveniently without forking out the high cost of cabs."

"I can't believe how different it sounds. And if you take into account it's actually just on the other side of the river."

Eli nodded, "*Jah*, but wasn't that the plan when our forefathers wrote the first *ordnung*? That we would be protected against *Englisch* influences, that we will keep the same foundations and way of living that we had years ago. I think it was a *gut* plan. If I see how technology and wealth can ruin lives… you might not understand it now, Joanna, but believe me, you're lucky to have lived here your whole life."

Joanna nodded, not knowing how to respond to that. They walked for a short while longer in silence before Eli finally stopped in another clearing. Together they searched the surrounding trees for a ribbon, but there was none to be found.

"I guess we found a clearing that you haven't searched yet."

Eli nodded. "Okay," said Eli, "Do you want to start over there?"

Joanna accepted the shovel he handed to her and looked around before she sunk the edge of the shovel into the firm dirt. "How deep do we have to dig?"

Eli shrugged, his shovel already buried to the hilt before he lifted it with a pile of dirt. He dumped the dirt beside him before turning to Joanna.

"I'm honestly not sure. I remember back then it felt like I was digging for ages, but you know how time seems to crawl by when you know you're somewhere you're not supposed to be. Probably no more than three feet deep, hopefully less."

Joanna began digging. The ground was mercifully easy to work. But despite their best efforts, they knew after an hour that there was nothing to be found. Eli tied a piece of ribbon on a tree and they walked on. Eli stopped for a brief moment to reach into the backpack he had grabbed when he collected the shovels. He took out two bottles of water and handed one to Joanna. "Drink up, don't want your headache to come back."

Joanna accepted the bottle with a smile but when their fingers touched the smile faded and her heart leapt…

Their gazes met and for a brief moment Joanna felt the connection she had felt at the barn raising. Was there something here worth exploring or was she just imagining it? Eli cleared his throat and stepped back.

"We best get a move on if we want to check another clearing before we head back."

Two hours and two more clearings later, they had

still not found anything. Joanna's back was protest-
ing against the hard work, but there was no way she
was going to tell Eli that he had been right, that this
was a man's work. She stood up and stretched her
back, with her arms in the air while Eli tied ribbons
to the trees.

Over the last thirty minutes she noticed him becoming frustrated. It was only her first day helping
him dig, but for Eli it had been almost two weeks.

"This is hopeless. I don't know why I ever started.
We're never going to find a wooden box barely a foot
long in a forest this size. Do you know how many
factors could have determined which way I went that
night? I might have run towards the light, or my one
tread might have been heavier, causing me to run
in a curve… It doesn't matter how many times I go
over it, it just doesn't look like we'll ever be able to
find the exact spot I found that night."

Joanna looked at Eli with pity. The poor boy. She
couldn't imagine what he must have gone through
over the years. His *daed* dying suddenly. It is one
thing with a family member being ill, allowing opportunity to prepare for their death; you can pray
to *Gott* together and seek comfort. But falling off
a barn roof with no warning, it must be terrible.
And then being uprooted from the only home you
ever knew to start again in a different culture with
people who didn't understand you. To top it all, the
feeling of regret for something that you did on the
spur of the moment with anger in your heart. She
wanted to help, she wanted to comfort, but she knew

she couldn't. Not yet. Not when they were alone like this.

"There is always hope, Eli. While we have *Gott*, we always have hope," Joanna said in a soothing voice. "There are a lot more clearings and we have two more months. We'll find it. You just have to believe."

Eli looked at Joanna with an empty expression. "But I don't know if I still have *Gott*."

"Of course you do, Eli," Joanna said. "You can't lose *Gott*. He is always there. You might just have to look deeper to find Him. Talk to Him, ask Him to help, ask Him to bring back your happiness and to make you feel that joy again. Hope is never lost."

Eli stood quietly for a moment watching her before he finally spoke in barely more than a whisper. "Will you pray with me? I never stopped praying but it's been a long time since someone prayed with me."

"Yes, Eli. Of course. *Gott* will show us a sign."

They took a seat on a fallen log and closed their eyes silently in prayer. After a few moments, Joanna opened her eyes and waited for Eli to finish praying.

Finally, Eli raised his head, "I feel calmer now. I just need to keep searching."

Joanna raised her own head with a smile. "That's exactly what I think *Gott* is trying to tell us. What does it say in Luke? *Ask and it will be given to you. Seek and ye shall find.*"

A huge smile erupted over Eli's face. "Well, in which case, we need to seek a little more." He paused and got to his feet. "But not today. We have been searching and digging for hours. And you need to get home; I don't want you to get into trouble again."

Joanna laughed as he struggled to come upright. "And maybe you might add how you're just a little bit tired and sore as well."

Eli shrugged with a crooked grin, "Might be, but I'll never admit it."

Joanna thought that the fact that he was thinking about her and not himself was very kind. Another great quality Eli seemed to have.

They walked back to Jacob's farm, talking about everything and nothing. And more than once, Joanna was convinced that Eli's eyes lingered longer than was necessary on her.

Was it possible that he had felt the connection as well? She didn't want to get her hopes up but secretly she believed she was right. When they were praying together in those woods, surely she would have known if spending time with Eli was wrong. She would have felt guilty or at least a little bad for seeing him when she knew her parents wouldn't approve.

She pushed the thought aside when they reached the edge of Jacob's property.

"*Kumm*, I'll walk home with you," Eli offered kindly.

Joanna considered for a moment before shaking her head. "I'll be fine. You go on home; your aunt and uncle are probably wondering where you've been. I know the way home."

She didn't add that she didn't want her parents to know that she had spent the afternoon with Eli Stoltzfus, and she didn't want to spoil that afternoon with her father scolding her.

Her family would be back soon, and she thought that if she was seen in the company of Eli quite so soon, there may be an argument.

Joanna almost skipped home, she felt so merry. After a wonderful afternoon with Eli, there was a slight tang of disappointment that he was having doubts about *Gott* and that they hadn't found the box. She vowed that she would pray hard every night until it was found. She hoped that Eli would make some form of peace with his past then.

As she approached her *haus*, she heard the familiar sound of a buggy trundling up the road behind her. The horse's clip-clop had a distinctive sound, and she knew immediately that it was Harry. She turned around just as her *familye*'s buggy rounded the corner. Jeremiah pulled on the reins, slowing the buggy as he drew closer before finally stopping. All three had grave looks on their faces, not the normal smiles after a day in town.

She instinctively knew something was wrong. She reached out and patted Harry's nose and he gave a low murmur of contentment.

"You are feeling better, then?" her mother asked after assessing her.

"Yes, thank you, *Mamm*. I went back to sleep for a while, and when I woke up the headache was almost gone. Those pills you gave me truly helped."

"*Gut*, I'm glad to hear you're feeling better. After today… I'm glad you're feeling better. Where've you been?"

Joanna smiled, glancing out over the hills. "I just took a short stroll in the air to clear my head completely. Did something bad happen in the town? " she asked, looking at their downcast faces.

Her mother turned to her father and Joanna knew the news was bad. Her mother was always eager to share news of a positive nature, but not so much the bad.

A heavy feeling settled over her as she turned to look at her father. Not even Jeremiah, who was always cheerful, was now smiling. Even he sat with his eyes downcast.

Her father sighed, climbing out of the buggy before moving towards Joanna. "*Nee*. Everything was fine in town. However, on the way back we ran into Ruth King. I'm afraid I've got some bad news. Young Sampson has developed pneumonia. The doctors say he is gravely ill," her father said with a serious expression.

Horror flooded Joanna's mind. She had been praying to *Gott* for the stupid idea of marriage to Sampson to be dropped. Could she somehow be responsible for Sampson's illness? She felt terribly guilty and concerned… What would happen if he died? She would never forgive herself. She would now have to pray to *Gott* for Sampson to recover and get well.

"But it was just flu. You said he had the flu?" Joanna heard the concern in her own voice and hoped her parents didn't misinterpret it for an unfounded interest in Sampson.

"It was, my *dochder*, it was. But sometimes flu has a way of taking a turn for the worse. I remember back before you were born, we had a cold winter that brought with it a terrible flu epidemic. We lost two elders that winter. It happens. Not often, thank *Gott*, but it happens."

Joanna slowly shook her head from side to side. Pneumonia was serious and if the doctors were worried, that made it all the more serious.

"Try not to worry too much," her mother consoled, leaning over the side of the buggy. "I know how fond you are of him."

Normally such a blatant misrepresentation of reality would incite an objection from Joanna, but she was still numb with the news and the worry that she was somehow responsible for Sampson's condition. She knew she hadn't prayed for him to get sick, but she couldn't help but feel guilty that she had been so against marrying him. It wasn't that she had now changed her mind; it was just a matter of being concerned over a healthy young man falling ill so suddenly.

"Come on," her *daed* said gently, climbing back into the buggy. "You can ride with us for the rest of the journey home. You seem to have gone pale."

Jeremiah reached out and helped Joanna climb on board. He patted her leg in a calming manner.

"I'm sure he'll be all right in the end. And then

you can arrange your marriage," he smiled reassuringly.

The words caused Joanna's head to spin and she felt faint. Yes, she obviously wanted Sampson to get well. But if he did, marriage seemed to be the likely outcome. It was too much. Too confusing. Tears started gently rolling down her cheeks.

"Now, now, dear," her *mamm* smiled, passing her a handkerchief. "Dry those eyes. In the morning you should go over and visit the Kings. Ask personally how Sampson is faring. See if you can do anything to help."

Joanna was too emotionally confused to disagree.

Chapter Seven

Sickness and Health

Joanna barely slept that night. All night long she tossed and turned, and when she finally found solace in sleep, she woke up sweating and shivering after a nightmare. In her dream she was standing over Sampson King's grave, very much like the day they stood over Eli's father's grave. But instead of mourning, the entire community was looking at her.

Knowing sleep wouldn't let her rest and the nightmares wouldn't cease, Joanna climbed out of bed and kneeled next to it.

"Gott, please be with Sampson. Please heal his disease-ridden lungs and make him healthy again. Please forgive me for not wanting to marry him, I never hoped for this to happen. If this was Your way of answering my prayers, I pray now that You heal Sampson, Gott. If it is Your wish that I should marry, Gott, I will do so. Just please, Gott..." her

voice broke with emotion and she quickly brushed away a tear. *"I ask Your healing and Your forgiveness, just please heal Sampson."*

When Joanna climbed back into the bed, she couldn't deny that the furthest from her wishes would be to marry Sampson King. Although she had vowed to marry him if that was what *Gott* chose, she couldn't help but admit that she harbored no affection for the young man.

She wasn't in love with him. She didn't even like him.

Guilt flushed over her at the thought after she prayed for *Gott* to heal Sampson. She pushed the thought away and crept deeper under the covers. Was love really necessary for a marriage?

The question had always seemed simple to her, until now.

She remembered her mother once telling her about the arranged marriage between her and her father. Her mother, a young girl living in Millersburg, Ohio at the time, had been paid a visit by the travelling match maker. She had arranged a match between Beatrice and Jared without the two ever having met. On the day of their wedding her mother had wept at being forced to marry a man in a strange community.

But the moment she saw Jared, she knew the match was perfect. Butterflies bounced in her tummy as her heart warmed. She grew to love Jared more than she ever imagined possible, and together they had lived a happy life. They had a *familye*, the farm and all the happiness they could have asked for.

Maybe a marriage to Sampson could work if she gave it a chance. As her *mamm* had said in the garden, the Kings were much respected in the community. Maybe Sampson had changed since he was a child. After all, Joanna had spent very little time with him over the last few years. Maybe he'd grown into a more affable young man. He was always very popular at the summer volleyball games; everyone seemed to like him there. Perhaps she was judging him harshly based on past experiences. But there was one picture that kept popping into Joanna's mind. A picture that caused doubt.

The picture of Eli chopping wood, working up a sweat in the late morning, so handsome and strong. The moment he looked up and smiled at her; in that moment her world tilted upside down and Joanna knew she was very much in love with her childhood friend.

Joanna would remain true to her prayers, but if Eli remained in the community and took a wife, she knew she would struggle with at least one of the seven deadly sins for the rest of her life.

Envy.

With all her heart and soul, Joanna believed Eli to be the *mann* for her, but she couldn't let Sampson suffer because she chose not to proceed with her parents' plans for her, and quite possibly *Gott*'s plan, too.

When the sun rose in the East, Joanna pushed

back the covers and climbed out of bed. She had barely slept a wink, but she couldn't spend another minute contemplating a situation she had no idea how to resolve.

Joanna didn't object at breakfast when her *mamm* insisted again that the first thing she should do that day was to go over to the King *haus* to ask after Sampson's health. Joanna wanted to see if *Gott* had taken action on her prayers overnight and had made Sampson well again. She knew it would seem to her parents that she was caving in on the idea of marriage. But at the moment there was little she could do on that front; her first concern had to be to ensure that Sampson got well again. After all, she was sure it was all her fault that he was sick in the first place.

Her *mamm* had been baking the previous evening and had prepared her specialty: blueberry streusel *kaffe* cake. She had put it in a basket together with honey bars for Joanna to take over to the Kings. Her *mamm* whispered in ear before she left that she might like to leave the impression that she herself had baked the goods. Joanna shook her head disapprovingly. Her *mamm* clearly wanted the Kings to think she was a good cook and that she had been thinking about Sampson, but Joanna had caused enough trouble as it was.

Besides, if the wedding went ahead, Sampson shouldn't be under the impression that she was as competent a baker as her mother. Joanna had many talents but unfortunately baking had never been one of them.

Before it even reached nine o'clock, Joanna was out on the road, walking up to the King *haus*, with the basket under her arm. Her pace was brisk, not because she was eager to spend time with Sampson but because she was eager to see if her prayers had by chance resulted in the miracle of him having received healing.

As she walked, she heard the sound of a buggy approaching from behind. She hoped that David King hadn't been forced to go into town to fetch the doctor; maybe Sampson had taken a turn for the worse during the night. She turned to find to her delight that it was Eli driving Jacob's buggy by himself. He immediately smiled and waved when he saw her. A warm feeling spread through her chest as a smile spread across her face.

As he approached, Eli slowed the buggy to a halt and then leaned down to speak to her.

"Hiya, Joanna," he beamed. "I didn't expect to see you out so early."

"Hiya, Eli," Joanna replied. She couldn't help but feel guilty that Eli had caught her on her way to see Sampson.

"You looked tired," he said cheerfully, "Did the headache return?"

Joanna stiffened, wishing she had taken more care of her appearance before she left the *haus*.

"I didn't sleep much, to be honest. But the headache hasn't returned, thank heavens. I see Uncle Jacob taught you to drive the buggy again. Where are you headed?"

"*Ach jah*. Jacob made sure I could drive a buggy within a week of my arrival. Said he wasn't playing chauffeur." An attractive grin spread across his face. "I have my car in town. Well, for the moment it is in Jacob's barn, but I wouldn't drive it around these parts."

"That's *gut*," Joanna said, glancing ahead. If David King came across her talking to Eli, he might get the wrong impression. A few weeks before she would have wished for it, but with Sampson ill, it was the last thing she wanted to happen.

"I'm heading into town to pick up a few things for Aunt Delia. Would you like to join me? I can maybe buy you a *kaffe*, if you're feeling up to it?" He took off his peak cap and dragged a hand through his hair, making Joanna wonder if he was ever going to wear plain clothes again. "Nothing improper of course."

Joanna would have liked nothing more than a buggy ride into town with Eli. Buggy rides with young *menner* actually meant something in the Amish community. And there would be little doubt that Eli hadn't forgotten what that was. But her face fell into a frown as she remembered what she had to do that morning.

"*Nee*, Eli. Unfortunately, I can't. I am going up to the King farm to see how Sampson is. He has pneumonia, you know," she added in barely more than a whisper.

Eli looked immediately put out. "*Nee*, I didn't know that," he replied quickly. "I didn't know you were friends, but you've always been a kind person, so I should have expected it."

I'm concerned because I believe I'm responsible, Joanna thought. If she had not prayed to *Gott* to prevent the marriage, none of this would ever have happened, she was convinced of it.

"I wouldn't say we're friends…" the words tumbled out because Joanna could not stop them. "What I mean is…"

"Joanna, tell me…" Eli urged with a frown.

"Our parents, Sampson's and mine, they have this idea of Sampson and I getting married."

Joanna didn't want to tell him, but she wasn't going to lie to him either. It was best if he knew the truth even if it caused the fallen expression on his face.

Eli raised his brows as he shook his head. "I'm sorry. I didn't realize, I didn't think you were courting," his voice was distant, a hint of anger clear.

"We're not courting," Joanna tried to explain. "It's just our parents are trying to match us, although I begged them not to…"

He looked angry, "I feel like a right idiot now. I would have never asked you to join me if I knew you were all but engaged."

Joanna immediately felt guilty and upset for having unintentionally hurt him. "*Nee*, Eli, it isn't like that. I promise it isn't. We aren't courting," she insisted. "It is *Mamm* and *Daed*, they're afraid I'm going to become a spinster and they came up with this plan…" she shook her head. "I don't even like him."

"So why are you going to see how he is?" Eli demanded, not really understanding the pressure her parents had put on her to behave appropriately in light of the situation.

"Because my parents say that I should, Eli. I've defied them enough over these last few weeks," she said, thinking how her *daed* had said that she shouldn't spend so much time with the *Englischer* who had just returned to the community.

Then the tears began rushing down her face and despite her efforts to stop them, they wouldn't, "And because I'm responsible for his illness." The words came out broken amidst the pitiful sobs, but she couldn't hold them back any longer.

"You are responsible for his illness?" Eli questioned with disbelief and horror. "How can that be? You said he had pneumonia." He reached into his pocket and found a clean handkerchief which he handed to Joanna. "Here. Wipe away your tears."

"Because I prayed to *Gott* to prevent the marriage from happening. I prayed that *Gott* would find a way to stop our parents' foolish idea, and the next thing Sampson was ill. It is all my fault; it has to be."

Eli's eyes softened as he climbed out of the buggy. He walked to Joanna and lifted her chin until she looked him in the eye. "Don't be *ferhoodled*, or even worse, a *dummkoppf*. Praying for *Gott* to help put an end to your parents' plans wouldn't land Sampson with pneumonia. He probably just had the flu and it took a turn for the worse. Sampson's illness is no doing of yours," he reassured her kindly.

Joanna nodded and wiped away her tears. She knew he was being kind, but it still didn't dispel her fears.

Eli sighed and shook his head before summoning a ghost of a smile. "If your parents think this is a *gut* decision for you, Joanna, perhaps you shouldn't fight them. The Kings are a reputable *familye*…" he trailed off and Joanna could see in his eyes that he didn't mean a single word of what he had just said.

Two lines formed between her brows as she frowned at his words. "You honestly believe that? That I should spend the rest of my life with Sampson King?" She shook her head completely taken aback. One minute he was proposing a buggy ride and coffee and the next he was telling her to marry a boy he very well should have known she had never liked. Eli was there on that fateful, life-affirming day in the woods; he knew how cruel Sampson could be.

Eli cleared his throat before nodding firmly, "If your parents believe that you should. They've always had good judgment in the past, haven't they?"

Joanna couldn't deny that. Her *daed* had always made good decisions. Maybe Sampson was the right person for her to marry. She shrugged her shoulders, not willing to concede the point.

Eli looked at her blue eyes, made even more pronounced by the tears, and he sighed. He had no idea why he was pushing her on the idea of marrying Sampson, but it felt like the right thing to do.

"At least consider it, Joanna. It would be disrespectful to just dismiss it."

Joanna nodded and Eli couldn't help the aching feeling that settled over his heart. He didn't want Joanna to marry Sampson King or anyone else for that matter. But in that moment, he realized how much she meant to him. The feelings that had started to grow between them since his arrival in Lancaster County had never been more pronounced than in that moment with Sampson King hanging over their heads.

He wanted to tell her to ignore her parents, to spend her life with him, but he was in no position to do anything of the kind. He didn't even know where he was going to spend his life, never mind with whom.

It was hard to admit it, but love made it easier. Eli knew he wasn't good enough for a girl like Joanna Lapp. She needed a proper Amish man who would stand by her side without doubts about his faith or where he wanted to spend his life. She needed someone she could love and care for, someone she could spend her life with, with whom she could raise a *familye*.

The last thing Joanna needed were his demons haunting her as well. It didn't help that the proposed marriage was to Sampson King. The day he found out about his father's passing, Eli couldn't help but blame the Kings just a little.

Why did they let his father climb onto that roof when it had obviously been about to rain? Couldn't they wait for the next day? He knew it was foolish to try and pin blame for an accident but that didn't make it any easier. For a moment he thought of all the men in the community who might be suitable to court Joanna, and he knew that no one would suffice. No one would be good enough for her, besides him.

It might be selfish but looking into Joanna's eyes Eli wanted something for himself for the first time in a very long time.

Joanna dried her eyes and handed him his handkerchief. "*Jah*. Maybe you are right, Eli. Maybe I should consider the matter a little more closely. Thank you for your advice. It has been a great comfort to me. I had better get up to the King's farm. Goodbye, Eli."

And with that she began marching up the road, away from Eli and towards Sampson King.

Eli watched her leave and shook his head. He wanted to chase after her and tell her that he loved her and wanted to be with her forever. But he couldn't. He was rooted to the spot. Now he had made matters worse. Not only did he not tell her how he really felt, but he had practically told her to go off and marry someone else.

He felt like an idiot.

Coming back to the community had been a disaster. You don't immediately find peace and tranquility after years of rushing around and mayhem. You can't just connect with *Gott* straight away after years of not praying. You can't just find a box of treasures you so stupidly discarded as a child. And, he decided, you can't fall in love with someone you only knew as a child. He wished he hadn't bothered coming back.

He climbed back on the buggy and drove off, clenching his jaw as he fisted his hands around the reins.

Perhaps it would be better for everyone if he just left today. The girl he loved was going to marry someone else; someone Eli didn't even like, and nothing else was going as planned. He thought of Joanna's words in the woods and closed his eyes and prayed. Hopefully this time *Gott* would listen.

Joanna listened as the buggy moved past her, but she didn't turn to look. She didn't want to give Eli the satisfaction of knowing that she cared when it was clear that he didn't care in the least. She had thought they had shared a connection, that something had happened between them in the woods, something so special that she had prayed that he would stay.

Now she wasn't certain he even cared about her at all. The only thing that had transpired from their conversation was that he didn't care. Not at all. How could he encourage her to marry Sampson? It was absurd and hurtful.

If everyone believed that she should marry Sampson, perhaps she should.

Would Sampson King really be that bad?

She asked herself a difficult question but answering it was even more difficult. If Sampson King was her only chance of having a *familye* of her own, would she reconsider?

She shook her head and knew the answer in her heart.

She wouldn't. She couldn't imagine having children with a man she didn't love. In the distance Eli's buggy grew ever smaller and she couldn't help but wonder if he was speaking from the heart or if the demons of the past were still haunting him. Is it because he didn't know where he wanted to spend his life that he told her to marry Sampson?

Joanna couldn't help but falter in her step at the thought. How could she possibly help Eli find the peace and the happiness he so desperately needed? Firstly, she knew that he needed to find the box that held all the buried memories of his father. Once he had that box, at least he could set that regret aside.

She could continue to search for his box, she didn't need his help. He had tied white ribbons in the clearings that he had already searched. She would simply tie ribbons in the clearings that she had searched as well. How would he know if they were the ribbons he had tied, or hers?

He wouldn't.

Although she was still angry with him, she felt better knowing she had a plan.

A short while later she opened the garden gate to the King's home. They had a very nice single-story home, that looked much larger than Joanna's home from the outside. The outbuildings were neatly kept, the barn boasted a freshly painted red roof. A smile curved her mouth at the pretty sight of the barn with the hills as a backdrop.

If she married Sampson, would they live here? She quickly pushed the thought aside and climbed the steps leading up to the front door. After three brisk knocks, she waited.

The door opened to reveal Ruth King.

"Hullo, Mrs. King," Joanna said with a warm smile.

Ruth King shook her head in disbelief. "Joanna Lapp, what a *gut* surprise. Come in, I'll make us some tea."

Joanna considered turning down the offer of tea but after the long walk she would appreciate a drink. She followed Ruth into the farm-style kitchen. The woodstove had heated the room and Joanna didn't have to peek into the pot to know that chicken soup was on the boil.

"What brings you all the way out here?" Ruth asked, joining Joanna at the table with the tea.

Joanna pushed forward the cake tin. "*Mamm* baked a little yesterday. I thought some honey bars might cheer Sampson up a little. How is he doing?"

A smile wrinkled the corners of Ruth's eyes, "That was a *wunderbaar* idea of yours, Joanna. I'm sure he'll be glad you came by. Unfortunately, he's sleeping just now."

Joanna nodded, "Is he better?"

The smile broadened before Ruth sighed, relieved, "*Jah*, he truly is. The doctor came by early this morning to look at him again; dear *mann* has been coming by every morning this week. He believes that Sampson has turned a corner and that from here things can only get better."

Joanna couldn't stop the smile that spread on her face, "That is *wunderbaar* news. I'm so happy. We were so concerned."

"I know. We were concerned as well. Last week when he struggled so desperately for breath…." Ruth trailed off before taking a deep breath. "But it's all over now. The doctor has him on all sorts of *Englisch* medication, but I won't complain. *Gott* wouldn't have given *mann* the talent to create medicine if he didn't want us to use it."

Joanna knew a few of the older generation in their community would argue that point, but she didn't. "I agree. *Mamm* sends her regards. She wanted to come with, but she has a few chores this morning that needed to be done."

Ruth laughed, "Chores…heaven only knows when I'll finally get to the laundry and the cleaning. With Sampson being ill, matters of that sort have slipped quite a bit, I'm afraid."

"I can help. I don't have anywhere to be this morning. I'd be happy to do whatever I can," Joanna offered with a smile. She knew how an untidy home and piles of laundry could weigh on a woman's mind and could clearly see that Ruth needed a little help to ease her conscience now that Sampson was recovering.

"Really? Ach *nee*, I can't expect you to help," Ruth waved the offer away.

"I insist. I'll clean the front rooms, which will leave you free to do the laundry. In a couple of hours your housework will be up to date again."

"You really are a *Gott* send, Joanna Lapp," Ruth smiled kindly.

Joanna was right. Within two hours the laundry was on the line and the front rooms all sparkled after a good dust and polish. She had hoped to see Sampson for herself but when Ruth checked again, he was still sound asleep. Joanna knew that sleep was the body's way of healing itself, so she asked Ruth to pass her best wishes on to Sampson when he was ready to receive them.

Joanna hoped that the walk home would clear her mind, but when she arrived back at her *haus* she was even more confused than before. She had very strong affections for Eli but after this morning she couldn't be sure he liked her at all. As for Sampson, could he truly be that horrible if his mother was such a nice woman? Perhaps that day in the woods so many years ago had simply been the sign of a child acting up rather than a true reflection of his character.

She stopped in front of their barn and decided to pay Harry a visit before joining the *familye* inside. Seeing the grey gelding took her thoughts once again to Eli. Would Eli really want her to marry Sampson? She shook her head, pushing all thoughts of Eli aside. Perhaps the best she could do was to allow Sampson to court her properly. She might then fall in love with him, or she might not. At the very least, though, she would know whether or not he possessed the character he had exhibited that fateful day in the woods, when the fox had determined Joanna's take on the nature of Sampson's soul.

Joanna sighed before heading out of the barn and into the kitchen. She wanted to do a few things before she could go to the woods this afternoon. Because, even if Eli wanted to be mean, she still cared about him. She was going to help him find that box whether he wanted her to or not. It was as simple as that.

Chapter Eight

The Mistake

When Eli awoke the next morning, he immediately knew he had made a terrible mistake. There was no way that Joanna should be considering having to marry Sampson. It didn't matter that her parents thought he would be a good match for her.

Marriage was sacred and should take place only between two people who truly loved each other. Not because their parents thought they'd be a good match. The thought of Joanna marrying Sampson now seemed simply preposterous to him. He couldn't help but admit that it wasn't because there was no love lost between him and Sampson; it was because there was more than plenty of love to be lost between himself and Joanna Lapp.

He knew that Joanna didn't want to marry Sampson; she had made that quite clear. Until that crucial meeting on the road, she had never mentioned

Sampson in all the time they had spent together, it was obvious there were no feelings there. Why should her parents be allowed to force her to marry a man for whom she had no feelings whatsoever? Eli knew that had been the way many years ago when the Amish communities were small, and they needed to mix up the bloodlines. But times had changed. Ohio had the biggest community of all, and Joanna's mother was from Ohio. Marrying Joanna suddenly seemed to Eli impossible not to be imperative.

For so many years he had searched for happiness in his past, and he still believed that if he found the memory box with his father's things, it would ease some of the guilt and the pain from the past, but Joanna was his future.

He had not a single doubt left in his mind.

He was surprised when he met her again at the barn raising; he simply assumed that she would be married by now, possibly with *kinners* of her own.

But she wasn't.

She didn't even have a boyfriend.

Over the last few weeks he had come to know Joanna as the kindhearted and obedient girl she had always been when they had been friends as *kinners*. She would make a wonderful mother and wife. Yesterday, envy and anger had caused him to say things he now regretted, but how could he go back on his words?

He had all but chased Joanna into the arms of Sampson King.

Shaking his head, Eli knew he had made the big-

gest mistake of his life the day before. He had no
idea how he was going to remedy it. But he couldn't
let Joanna marry a man she didn't love. They hadn't
expressed their feelings for one another, but Eli was
certain she was more than attracted to him. Why
else would she smile brightly whenever she saw
him? What other reason could there be for her to
help him search for his father's memory box?

He brooded and sulked like a spoiled child for the
next week. Each morning he would work out in the
yard, hoping against hope that Joanna would come
by. But she never did.

In the afternoons he would harness the horse and
buggy and ride past Joanna's *haus* in the hopes of
perhaps coming across her on the road, or perchance
finding her reading a book on the porch.

But again, he never did. Twice he was on the
verge of stopping at the *haus* and knocking on the
door, but each time he decided against it. He strongly
suspected that her *daed* heavily disapproved of him,
being what he considered an *Englisch* man. Besides,
if he showed up at the Lapp home it would make
his intentions of courting Joanna as clear as crystal
to all and sundry.

He thought it would be best to see Joanna in
private first, to declare his feelings. If she was
agreeable, then he would confirm his return to the
community and be baptized.

He would wear the plain clothes Aunt Delia had
given him during that first week of his arrival. The
thought of spending the rest of his life in Lancaster

County didn't frighten him as he once thought it might. In fact, was that relief that washed over him? No more chasing deadlines, no more technology, no more fast-paced weeks; only chores and a humble job.

What would he do for work?

Over the last few weeks he had been helping Uncle Jacob in the carpentry business, but he was nowhere near the skilled carpenter his father had been. But perhaps…perhaps if he proved himself as a worthy member of the community and a skilled carpenter, he could care for his *familye*.

Maybe then Joanna's *daed* would approve and grant them his blessing to get married. But if he was not able to even see Joanna, he couldn't possibly speak to her. He knew that Sampson King was getting better. Uncle Jacob had mentioned running into David King the day before. Although it would take time for Sampson to recover completely, he was very certainly on the mend. If Sampson was on the mend, then he would soon be well enough to receive visitors. Eli knew who would be visiting him for sure.

While he fought his own conflicting emotions, he still took time every day to search for the memory box. He couldn't even remember the number of holes he had dug over the last month, and yet he was no closer to finding it than when he had first started on his mission of rediscovery.

Many were the times he lay in bed and tried to figure out where he would have run that night;

where the clearing might be; anything that would set it apart from elsewhere in the woods. But nothing.

It didn't help that whenever he stepped into the woods, he thought of Joanna. It also didn't help that he was beginning to lose direction every time he ventured into the wooded area.

When he first started to search for the missing box, he began at the edge of the woods and worked in a northerly direction. Many where the times now that he came across a clearing that he had marked but had no memory of having searched himself.

Perhaps it was the stress, perhaps thoughts of Joanna were muddling his mind, but he kept searching for new clearings to dig.

He had taken the time to pray to *Gott* to help him resolve all his problems. Joanna had thought it would help and he really wanted to find his connection to *Gott* again after all these years. He prayed hard. *Gott* would answer his prayers, wouldn't He? He simply had to have faith.

After seven days without seeing Joanna, Eli decided enough was enough. He had slept fitfully, but he kept dreaming of a clearing with flowers. Pale yellow flowers. He awoke early with the conviction that this was a sign from *Gott*. He crept into the kitchen so as not to wake Jacob and Delia too early. He left them a short, scribbled note to let them know not to worry and that he would be back before nightfall. He began his lonely walk to the woods just as the sun was rising. The view was stunning;

it seemed to be just the glorious spring morning on which to resolve his issues.

He had his backpack of food and drink to sustain him throughout the day. He would walk until he found the clearing that had appeared in his dream; he would dig and then he would certainly find his box. He had no doubts about that now. And then he would take the buggy and drive himself down to Joanna's *haus*. If her *daed* answered the door, he would be honest and forthright and explain his intentions. If Joanna told him that he wasn't welcome, he would leave the Amish community for good. But one way or the other, today would be the day he would resolve all that required his attention.

Eli walked ever deeper into the woods; down to the stream where he remembered playing with Joanna and the other *kinners* as a boy. The old rope swing was still in place, no doubt now being used by a new generation of *kinners*. He remembered one particular incident during which Sampson King had caught some kind of small animal in a trap and then proceeded to torture it until Eli had stepped in. He remembered how Joanna had argued with Sampson, telling him to free the injured animal. But Sampson had refused, and Joanna had run away in tears.

How could he stand by and let Joanna marry such a person as that?

He leapt over the stream in one stride. It was funny how it had seemed so much wider as a child. He walked quickly through the clumps of trees on the other side before coming to another clearing.

Again, he remembered this one as a child. He and Joanna would lie on their backs and watch the clouds float by in this very spot. They would tell each other what they saw in the clouds. Sometimes it was a horse's head, other times a buggy, sometimes an old man. Eli would often see Joanna's pretty face, but he would be too shy to tell her that.

Looking around the clearing now, he froze. Beneath the trees, he saw daffodils growing. None were yet in full bloom, but they were on the verge of bursting into life, so the delicate yellow of their petals was hard to make out. But Eli knew that this was the place.

He had begged *Gott* to help him, to send him a sign, and His sign was right before his eyes.

The yellow flowers.

Very excitedly he dropped the bag on the floor and proceeded to dig around the edge of the clearing using his shovel. When he came up empty after the first hole, he continued to the next, and the next until his back was straining under the exertion.

Eli took a quick break before he began again on the other side of the clearing. It took him most of the morning, with sweat drenching his T-shirt, but he didn't give up. *Gott* had sent him a sign and it had to be here some place.

He dug around the entire perimeter but there was no sign of the box anywhere. Eli threw the shovel down in frustration and sat down for a long drink of water. He stood up and surveyed the scene around him in earnest.

His jaw dropped as he slowly shook his head from side to side.

To his horror he saw daffodils everywhere in the woods, all bursting open, welcoming the warm rays of the sun. The dream hadn't been a sign after all. It was probably a trick played on him by his sub-conscious mind. He must have noticed the daffodils yesterday while he was digging, and they were now appearing in his dream just to trick him.

The daffodils had focused his concentration for the first time in weeks. He had not found his fa-ther's box and was ready to admit that he probably never would, but he had found something else in Lancaster.

He had found the woman he loved.

Joanna would not marry Sampson, of that he would make sure. He might not be great at finding things buried years ago, but he just knew he'd have better luck at finding Joanna and finally declaring his feelings to her.

He turned and practically ran back to the farm buildings, leaving his shovel and the bag behind in his haste.

He wasted no time in harnessing Jacob's old horse to the buggy.

"Do you fancy a fast canter, Dale?" He asked, taking the reins. "I need to get somewhere quickly. Will you help me?"

The old horse responded to Eli's request and he wasted little time in getting to Joanna's *haus*. He took a few seconds to compose himself before climbing from the buggy and forcing himself to walk at a normal pace up the stairs.

He heard footsteps inside which were approaching the door in response to his knock, Joanna's *mamm*, Beatrice, answered the door, her hands covered in flour.

"Eli?" she said with undisguised surprise. "I'm sorry for opening the door in this condition," she continued, waving her white hands in the air. "I'm baking bread. How can I help you today?"

Before Eli had a chance to answer, the door was pulled open further and Joanna's *daed,* Jared, filled the gap, his face fixed with a stern looking expression.

"Eli?" Jared didn't even bother to greet him; the silence was filled with all the unsaid words Eli could infer from the negative expression on his face.

Eli wouldn't be scared away that easily. "Hullo. I'm sorry to bother; I was hoping to have a word with Joanna?" He kept his tone cheerful and his smile in place although his words were met with confusion and anger respectively.

"*Nee*. She left quite early this morning; she said she would be out all day. I rather suspect she's gone to visit young Sampson King. The two are courting, you know?" Jared said with a smirk, obviously pleased to be the one to impart the news.

The words hit Eli like a punch to the stomach. He had most definitely not expected to hear that Joanna had gone to see Sampson King yet again. Had he misinterpreted her words? No, he was sure he hadn't. He also was not about to let Joanna's father scare him away just because he didn't fit into the plans he had made for his daughter. He decided he would be a little bolder.

"*Nee*. I didn't know. In fact, just a few days ago she told me that she wasn't being courted by Sampson at all. That she had no interest in marrying him, although you and his parents in conjunction seemed to be forcing the two of them to marry without even so much as a courtship."

Jared and Beatrice shared a look before Jared turned to Sampson with daggers in his eyes.

"I see. You see my *dochder* on a regular basis, do you?" demanded Jared. "Well, since we're being frank, it's my turn. I explicitly forbade Joanna to see you. I know you were friends as *kinners,* Eli, but back then things were different. For one, you were Amish. You've been here for more than a month and you're still wearing *Englisch* clothes. How can I let my *dochder* spend time with a *mann* who doesn't even know where he's going to be a month or two from today? I spoke to your uncle, Eli. He made it quite clear that you haven't decided to join the community." Beatrice touched her husband's arm in an effort to silence him.

"Eli, I'm sorry. Jared is just a little off color this morning," Beatrice tried with a soothing tone. "Although I know Joanna was reticent at the thought of marrying Sampson at first, I think his illness has cleared her mind. Sampson is a very handsome young *mann*, good stock from a *familye* that has farmed these parts for centuries. I think Joanna realized that she wouldn't find a better match elsewhere. I hope we can count on you to respect her decision?"

For a moment Eli considered agreeing and walking away, but he couldn't. Not from Joanna. That very morning, surrounded by nothing but woods and daffodils, it had struck him like a hammer blow between the eyes. He was hopelessly in love with Joanna and he wasn't going to back down now, not after having been fortunate enough to have found her again.

"I respect that you don't like me. I respect that I've been away from the community for eight years, but I'll remind you that it wasn't by choice. When I came back to Lancaster County it was to find out some truths for myself, to find out who I really am. Instead, I found the girl who used to be my best friend. I can promise that I will respect her decision, but I won't lie to you. I'm going to find Joanna and then I'm going to tell her that I love her."

Beatrice gasped, clutching her husband's arm.

Jared stepped forward, thunder flashing in his eyes. "You will do no such thing."

"I will. I know you won't believe me, Mr. Lapp, but I have changed. Coming back here has reminded me about all that is important in life. Our *ordnung* abides by two pillars: faith and *familye*. I want your daughter to be my *familye* because she helped me regain my faith. I know you won't understand but in time I'll prove to you that this is the right decision."

Eli didn't wait for a response this time; instead, he turned and rushed back towards his buggy.

Jared and Beatrice just stared at the disappearing buggy with shocked expressions on their faces. "I think there is going to be trouble," Beatrice said matter-of-factly before closing the door.

Eli didn't plan on gate-crashing a courting session but frankly he didn't care if he did just that. If that's what it took to tell Joanna how he felt about her, then that's what he'd do.

It didn't take Eli long to drive to the King's farm. He took a deep breath as he knocked on the door, knowing he was about to cause a whole world of trouble.

Mrs. King opened the door with a broad smile. "Eli, how nice to see you. Didn't expect you to come by. I heard you were back."

Eli nodded. He didn't have time for pleasantries right now even though Mrs. King had been friends with his mother before they left eight years ago. "I've been meaning to, it's just been…complicated. I was wondering if I could have a word with Joanna."

Mrs. King's brows drew together. "Joanna? Joanna Lapp? I'm afraid you have the wrong *haus*, Eli."

"*Nee*, her parents mentioned she was coming to see Sampson," Eli explained.

Her head slowly moved from side to side. "I'm afraid she isn't here. She only came to see us once last week when she brought the honey bars for

Sampson. She hasn't been here again. Is something wrong, Eli? You seem a little distressed."

Eli frowned, confusion slowly seeping into his mind. Why would Joanna tell her parents she and Sampson were courting if they clearly were not? Where was she if she told her parents she had come to see Sampson?

"*Denke*, Mrs. King. I'm sure it's just a mistake on my part."

Mrs. King nodded and bid him a good afternoon before closing the door. This time Eli didn't race to the buggy. He walked decisively, trying to figure out what had just happened.

Where could Joanna be? Had she honestly told her parents that she was going to see Sampson, or was that just a story her father told him to make sure he didn't come visit again? He pushed the thought aside, not believing that Jared would lie simply to keep Joanna from seeing him.

Then he remembered the anger in Jared's eyes. Jared would do anything to protect his daughter, including telling a lie. He climbed onto the buggy, confused and more than a little put out. Luck was definitely not on his side. The day he wanted to tell Joanna that he loved her, was the very day he couldn't find her. It was only early afternoon but to Eli it felt as if the day would never end. His stomach growled and he realized he hadn't even had breakfast that morning. Before he did anything else, it was time to head home and eat.

Driving home, he couldn't stop thinking about

Joanna. Was she lying to him, or had she been lying to her parents about going to see Sampson?

For all he knew she was now keen on the idea of marrying Sampson following his own behavior before.

He took the reins and directed the horse towards the Stoltzfus farm with a heavy sigh.

Chapter Nine

Sampson

Joanna promised herself that she didn't lie, as she trudged through the woods. Was it really a lie when you simply gave the impression of doing something and then did something else?

Alright, she admitted, it might be a lie.

But how else could she explain to her parents that she spent almost every afternoon in the woods searching for a hidden box that Eli had buried years before? When she hinted at going to the King farm, not Sampson specifically, both her parents had been overjoyed at the prospect. In fact, her mother had packed her a basket every day. The honey bars, cakes and fruit were her sustenance during the hard day's digging.

When her *mamm* wasn't looking, she slipped in a few bottles of water as well. She did feel guilty about what she was doing, and she knew her parents would find out in the end that she hadn't been to see Sampson, but hopefully that day wasn't today.

When they found out she would simply explain to them what she had been doing. She knew she was looking for a world of trouble, but she needed to find that box. Somehow over the last week that box had come to mean more to her than she ever imagined. It was as if finding that box would not only bring Eli peace, but it would bring her a future that she could look forward to.

Over the last few days she had become an avid digger. On the first day she had borrowed a shovel from her father's shed before heading into the woods. Not wanting to seem at all suspicious, she had left the shovel in the woods beside a tree stump she passed every day. It was a simple solution and it did help not having to carry the shovel back and forth daily.

In her mother's sewing basket, she found the same white ribbon Eli had used, and placed it in her apron.

Every clearing she unearthed, she made sure she searched thoroughly. The last thing she wanted was to mark a clearing as being searched only to have missed Eli's precious memory box. When she was done with a clearing, she would tie three ribbons around the trees at the edge of the clearing, knowing that Eli wouldn't search there again.

At night when she returned, she couldn't let her parents see how tired she was. She kept her smile in place and helped her mother with dinner and laughed at Jeremiah's jokes until it was time for her to drop into bed without raising suspicions as to her uncharacteristic weariness.

As soon as she was alone in her room, she would pray for *Gott* to help her find the memory box. But despite her prayers day in and day out, she had no success.

In her mind she knew it was a simple process of elimination: search a clearing, mark it and move on to the next, but it wasn't that simple in reality. In reality it was hard work, harder than anything she had ever done in her short life. Her arms and back were sore from hunching over and digging all the holes, her legs tired from walking the woods for most of every day, but she didn't let that stop her. If the box was meant to be found, then *Gott* would find a way for it to be found. Even if she had to dig up every clearing in the woods, she would. To give Eli peace of mind, she believed the box had to be found.

Joanna tried to explain her hard work and effort away as a determination to bring peace to Eli, but in the back of her mind she knew the truth. She hoped that once she found his sacred box, she could bring back his joy. She could explain to him that she wasn't interested in Sampson and would find a way for her parents to respect her feelings. That was yet another bridge to cross when she finally and inevitably got there.

But if she could, then she and Eli would be allowed to court. Perhaps if he fell in love with her in the same way she already was with him, he would realize that he was meant to return to the community. That he was meant to be Amish and not an *Englischer* chasing after worldly possession.

Alone in the woods she had plenty of time to think, and even more time to rethink all she had thought about before. She had already phrased the words in her mind that she would use to tell Eli if she saw him, but for now she kept her distance. She knew more or less where he was digging and always made sure not to be in the same area. The last thing she wanted was to see him when he was still angry at her for going to see Sampson.

If only he knew she didn't even get to see Sampson at all. If only she could tell him that she had only dusted and polished the King home to help Mrs. King.

She walked to the woods every day, skirting by the back of his uncle's home, careful not to be seen. Once or twice she caught sight of Eli chopping wood in the yard. More than once she wanted to go to him and explain how she felt.

But she couldn't, not until she was certain he wasn't angry and not until she knew he had a reason to stay. Foolishly she hoped she would be his reason for never returning to his previous life in Harrisburg. It was nothing but a stupid dream, but it was one that motivated every step, every swing of the shovel and every bead of sweat.

On the upside, she was becoming much more adept with a shovel. In the beginning a single hole had taken her nearly thirty minutes, now she managed that in just ten.

She had learned to use her legs all the better to drive the shovel into the dirt instead of pushing down with her arms, which required a lot more strength. Even though her technique had improved, it was still hard work. When she finally found a clearing that hadn't been marked yet, Joanna began digging. She started at the perimeter of the clearing and worked her way to the inside. It took her an hour to completely dig the perimeter of the clearing, yet again it produced nothing. She took a ten-minute rest, had a drink and ate a honey bar before she moved on to the next clearing. But just as she was about to take the first bite of the cake, she heard leaves crunch beneath a footfall. Certain it was just her imagination, she was about to ignore it when she heard a twig snap.

Joanna jumped up, fear clutching at her throat as she turned towards the sound. She noticed a large figure coming through the woods towards the clearing.

There had been no trouble in the woods that she could recall, but you never knew until you were faced with it. With the shovel as her only form of protection, Joanna grabbed it and held it over her head. It was then that the figure suddenly stopped, and recognition dawned in her mind.

"Sampson?" Joanna asked, shocked and confused all at once. "What on Earth are you doing here? You're meant to be ill."

Although he was pale and a little thinner after weeks of bed rest, the scowl on his face still frightened Joanna just a little.

"So, where is he?" Sampson demanded, stepping into the clearing.

"What are you talking about? Sampson, you look very pale, should you even be out here?" Joanna dropped the shovel and carefully stepped in his direction.

"The *Englischer*, Joanna, where is he?" Sampson's scowl hardened as he looked suspiciously around the perimeter of the clearing. "Don't lie to me, Joanna; I know you're hiding him somewhere. I've seen both of you come in here almost every day."

"What on Earth do you mean, Sampson?" Joanna asked, feeling afraid. Sampson was obviously incredibly angry, and here she was, all alone in the woods with no one to cry out to for help. This was the very same person she had watched hurt an animal for the pure fun of it as a boy, when he had not even been angered. She looked nervously towards the edge of the clearing and wondered if he would be fast enough to catch her if she decided to make a run for it.

He laughed wryly and shook his head before walking right up to Joanna. He stopped merely a foot from her, and his face contorted with disgust.

"You come to my *haus*; you bring me cakes and help my mother with her chores. You give her the impression that you're agreeable to accepting me as your husband and yet for the last week almost every day I've seen you and that *Englischer* sneak into the woods. I'm no one's fool, Joanna," he seethed through clenched teeth.

Fear trickled down Joanna's spine, causing a hollow feeling to grow in the pit of her stomach.

"Sampson…" she began, realizing only then the extent of what he had said. Confusion bloomed in her mind as she shook her head slowly. "You mean Eli? I haven't even seen Eli for over a week. What are you talking about?"

"Lies!" Sampson shouted, his voice causing her to jump. "I've seen you both and I've worked out your little plan. For three days I've watched you from my bedroom window. Did you know that my bedroom window overlooks the edge of the woods? It wasn't hard to recognize you. You are the only girl hereabouts with such fair hair, and no other *menner* hereabouts wears *Englisch* clothes," he said triumphantly as though that settled it.

"You always walk carefully around the back of his uncle's farm and then you disappear into the woods. Then a short while afterwards, the *Englischer* follows. He takes a different path, of course. Why else would you be coming to the woods if not to meet? Don't take me for a fool, Joanna. The only thing you can be doing is meeting him here in secret. When you are soon to be my fiancée! Do your parents know? This is highly improper. The *ordnung* does not permit…"

"I know perfectly well what the *ordnung* permits,

denke, Sampson King," Joanna cut him short, becoming angry herself.

How dare this man accuse her of impropriety? Who did he think he was, anyway? It was interesting that Eli was coming to the woods, though. It wasn't really a surprise, she fully expected him to be searching for his box as well. Just because he was angry at her, would be no reason to give up. The only surprise to her was that she hadn't heard or seen him in the woods at any time while she was searching. Sampson had obviously seen them from his bedroom window and immediately jumped to the wrong conclusion.

"Sampson, I have not been meeting Eli in the woods. As you can see, he is nowhere to be seen," Joanna insisted, waving her hand around her. "Or do you want to search behind every tree to see if he is there?"

"Then, what have you both been doing?" Sampson asked, now a little unsure of his ground since Eli was very clearly not with her.

"I suspect we've both been doing the same thing," replied Joanna, not really wanting to tell Sampson. It was, after all, none of his business. But she felt that she had very little choice, seeing the situation she was in, and being all alone. "Only we are certainly not doing it in each other's company. As you can well see for yourself, Sampson. Before Eli left the community, just after his *daed* died falling from your roof, he buried a box of personal treasures."

It was a low blow mentioning the fact that Eli's

father had died working on the King's barn, but she felt that Sampson deserved it for making her as scared as he had just a few minutes before.

"It has been destroying him knowing that he discarded it on impulse, in anger. Understandably, he wants to find it again. I've been digging in these clearings, looking for it. The fact that you say he's been disappearing to the woods as well means that he's probably been doing exactly the same. Digging for a little box of memories of his dead *daed*. Not coming to secretly meet me."

Sampson hung his head, clearly beginning to feel a little ashamed of the accusations he had been throwing about. "I thought…"

"Clearly you shouldn't think because you're not very good at it. And to clarify one more thought you might have had, my parents forced me to come and see you. I did not come because I wanted to give your mother the wrong impression. Of course, I was relieved to hear you were improving, that's only natural." Especially when you have been praying to *Gott* to prevent a marriage and you think it is all your fault, she thought. "But let me assure you, I gave no impression at all that I was keen on a possible match with you. *Jah*, I know our parents have our whole future planned for us. A wedding in fall, the first *boppli* by next summer…that is not what I want, Sampson. It just seems that it doesn't matter how many times I try to explain to them that I'm not interested in marrying you, they won't listen."

Sampson frowned for a moment before his face split in two with a foolish grin. "Really?"

Joanna nodded, slightly confused. Why would Sampson be smiling when she basically just made it clear that she had no intention of ever marrying him.

He burst out laughing and shook his head. "You don't want to marry me?"

Joanna nodded again. He wasn't supposed to be laughing or perhaps he was getting some perverse pleasure in knowing that she would be wed against her will.

"*Nee*, Sampson. I don't want to marry you. I don't even know you well enough, not to mention that I don't so much as like you. For the past five years I've barely seen you and what I saw while we attended school…" she trailed off not wanting to bring up the matter of the fox. "Let's just say I'd rather be an eternal spinster than your bride." She nodded firmly, making it clear that was how she felt.

Sampson laughed again, disbelief clear in his eyes. "This is the best news I've had in weeks, Joanna." Sampson roared with pleasure, "I don't want to marry you either."

"What?" Exclaimed Joanna. "You don't?" For all intents and purpose, it had seemed as if Sampson was delighted with his parents' plan for him to wed her.

"*Nee*. I don't. It's nothing personal really, I'm sure you're a wonderful girl and will make a *gut* mother. It's just that I love someone else."

For the first time in her life she saw Sampson's

eyes soften as a smile played on his mouth. "I'm in love with Ruth Beiler. I know she's older than I am, I know my parents probably won't approve, but I am. Ever since they told me about the arranged marriage they had all planned for us, I've been trying to find a way to set them straight. But my respect for your father and mother...all that kind of held me back."

"Did you tell your parents?" Joanna asked, excited at the prospect of putting this whole mess behind her.

"*Nee*. When I tried to tell them that I was already courting, they dismissed it and told me you were a better match. Like we're cows or something, it's actually ridiculous."

"I know. I honestly believe in the *ordnung* , but surely they can stop with the arranged marriages. Most of the older people have let that go, but not our parents."

"*Jah*. Besides, I thought you were eager, and I didn't want to let you down as well without talking to you. But then I got the flu and it all just sort of escalated from there." Sampson breathed a huge sigh of relief and sat down on the ground. "I don't think you know how relieved I am right now."

Joanna sat down too, also a little stunned at the revelation.

She noticed a group of daffodils blooming beside them and frowned when Sampson reached for them.

He very delicately picked one at the stem and held it up to Joanna. "Here, for you. A sign of my appreciation!" he joked.

Joanna smiled at the simple gesture. She sat down next to him, taking the daffodil out of his hand. "So, we have both been worried for nothing?" she inquired, seeing how funny the situation really was.

"It would seem so," replied Sampson. "After all, they can't really force us to marry if neither of us wants to, can they? It would be highly embarrassing for them to arrange the wedding and to get the whole community to come, only for us both to refuse to go through with the ceremony!"

"You would do that?" Joanna asked, surprised that he would go against his parents' wishes in front of the bishop and the entire community.

"I would," Sampson said firmly. "Especially knowing you weren't fond of the idea either."

"It wouldn't get that far, though," Joanna said, "We'd simply tell the bishop and he would refuse to even publish."

Sampson suddenly erupted into a fit of coughing. He bent over, clutching his hand to his abdomen as the coughing grew worse. When he finally managed to catch his breath, he looked at Joanna with a crooked grin. "Stupid pneumonia."

"Are you okay?" Joanna asked with concern, handing him an unopened bottle of water.

"Yes, I'm fine," Sampson insisted. "Just the back end of this terrible pneumonia. I've been stuck in my room for so long; I had to get out for some air. As I thought you were imminently about to become my fiancée and I saw you disappearing into the woods with the *Englischer* following straight afterwards,

I rather thought I should come down and find out what on Earth was going on." A wide grin appeared. "It turns out nothing was going on, and even better than that, you are not going to be my fiancée!"

Joanna couldn't help but laugh at the relief in his voice. As she watched Sampson laugh, she thought that maybe he wouldn't have been quite that bad as a husband. He was certainly handsome, although the illness had caused him to lose a fair amount of weight, leaving him looking thin and drawn. Then her mind went back to Eli and she felt guilty.

Sampson stood up, "You have had no luck in finding this mystery box, then?" he asked, waving his arm around the clearing.

"*Nee*," Joanna replied. "Not yet, but I have faith that I will." She smiled, this time with all her heart. *Gott* had answered her prayers when it came to Sampson's health and now when it came to the arranged wedding. Surely He would help them find the box as well.

Sampson started coughing again. "I would offer to help, but I think I should get back. I don't think a stroll in the woods is what the *Englisch* doctor had in mind when he told me to take it slow for a few weeks."

Joanna smiled, still holding the flower he had given her. "*Kumm*," she glanced around the clearing, knowing she should actually stay and search for the box. But she couldn't let Sampson go home alone looking as pale and as weak as he was. "I'll walk with you."

"Are you sure? I wouldn't want to impose. I can see how important this box…and the *Englischer* are to you."

Joanna frowned at his words. Maybe Sampson wasn't all she had thought him to be all along. Maybe he had changed and maybe she had been right on that fateful day with the fox, that he was merely a child acting out.

"Besides, how would you explain me dead in the woods?" He chuckled for a moment before he coughed again.

Joanna laughed. "You're right; best get you back to bed before I have a lot more explaining to do."

Once Joanna had tied a ribbon to the trees surrounding the clearing, she collected her basket and headed to where Sampson was waiting. "Ready?"

He nodded and they began walking.

They fell into step next to each other, Joanna slowing her pace to match Sampson's. They walked in silence, Joanna keeping a close eye on him every time he coughed. Just as they exited the thickest brush, Sampson stopped to catch his breath.

"I've been thinking. Maybe you should come home with me?"

Joanna's eyes widened. Hadn't they just settled the matter about the arranged marriage? The last thing she wanted to do was give his mother any more false impressions.

"Not like that," Sampson shook his head. "I think we should tell my parents that we don't want to get married. If we do it together, we can explain that we arranged to meet in the woods first of all, otherwise how will I explain that? And secondly, do you really think they'll force us to get married if they know neither of us wants to? I know they're old fashioned, but they're not mean."

Joanna tugged her bottom lip between her teeth. Maybe Sampson was right. He knew his parents better than she did and she'd much rather try and persuade his parents than her own. If they went together to speak her parents, too, the first thing her father would ask was whether this was because of the *Englischer* .

"*Jah*, perhaps if you're feeling up to it, when we're done, we could go see my parents as well. Get it all over and done with before the sun sets."

Sampson smiled taking the basket from her like a true gentleman. "Careful, Joanna, if you continue being so sensible, I might just insist on this wedding after all."

An hour, even thirty minutes ago, his words would have scared her, but somehow in that clearing in the woods Joanna became comfortable with Sampson and knew he was just joking.

Joanna felt a little nervous at the prospect of talking to Sampson's parents, but it seemed the sensible thing to do.

"*Jah*. That would be a *gut* idea. Perhaps you could rest a while at your *haus*, and then we might be able to go and see my parents together as well. Get it all over and done with in one go."

Once they cleared the edge of the woods, they

headed straight past Jacob's farm. Joanna kept an eye out for Eli, but there was still no sign of him, and they strolled slowly up the hill towards Sampson's *haus*.

The Kings were very welcoming when they arrived. They all sat down in the kitchen for *kaffe* and cake.

"So where have you two been?" Mrs. King asked once everyone was seated.

Sampson glanced at Joanna who nodded her consent. "We met to talk about the upcoming wedding," Sampson began.

"That's *wunderbaar*," Mrs. King clapped her hands in glee. "Do you have a date in mind?"

Joanna held her breath waiting for Sampson to break the news. He slowly shook his head. "*Nee,, Mamm*, we don't, because we don't want this wedding to happen."

It was Mr. King who spoke first after a few moments of silence. "Why is that?"

"Because neither Joanna nor I have that kind of affection for each other. We both want to marry someone we love, to spend our lives cherishing our partners, not simply tolerating each other because you planned the courtship."

Mrs. King was clearly upset by the news, but she nodded with a heavy sigh. "It was just so perfect. Sampson and Joanna. People have been suggesting it for years… I guess we just got caught up because neither of you seemed to be courting without help from us."

Sampson cleared his throat and took a deep breath. "Actually, I've been courting Ruth Beiler, *Mamm*, you just didn't ask."

Mr. King laughed, shaking his head, "And here I thought I had to have a word with my son about the fairer sex."

Sampson shook his head. "I was going to tell you before we went for dinner at the Lapps' but then the flu happened, and everything just spiraled out of control."

"It's alright," Mrs. King smiled first at Sampson and then turned to Joanna. "Really, we wouldn't want you to do something you'll regret. This is the rest of your lives you're talking about. If you're going to make a mistake, it would be best you make it on your own terms."

Joanna couldn't stop the smile that tugged at the corners of her mouth. "*Denke* for being so understanding. We weren't sure…"

"Ach…don't be *ferhoodled*. Of course, we understand. Have you spoken to your parents yet?"

"*Nee*," Sampson answered. "We're hoping to head there now."

"Are you up to it, Sampson?" his father asked, concerned.

Sampson nodded. "I bet I'll be tired when I get back, but I believe it's better we get it over with. Ready?"

Joanna nodded. "Ready as I'll ever be." She tried to summon a smile as nerves coiled in her belly. She didn't think her own parents would be as understanding of the whole matter as the Kings had just proven to be.

She said her farewells and thanked them for their kindness and then Sampson joined her outside. They decided that as it was just starting to get dark, the buggy would be the quicker way to get to Joanna's *haus*, and he began the process of harnessing the horse. Joanna thought of Eli, and the chest and the search in the woods while Sampson worked. Looking down at the daffodil in her hand, she smiled. She couldn't wait to see all the daffodils in full bloom. A smile curved her mouth when suddenly she let out a cry.

"I know! I know!" she cried, directing her gaze at the daffodil that was still in her hand.

"You know what?" asked a perplexed Sampson standing beside an even more confused horse.

"I know where Eli's missing box is!" Joanna announced with a broad smile splitting her face in two.

"Where?" Sampson asked stepping towards her. "You've searched almost every clearing there was to search."

Joanna shook her head. "*Jah*, we searched every clearing, but we didn't search in the right places. I'm sorry, Sampson, I can't go with you to see my parents. I have to do this while I am certain that I know where it is."

Sampson looked at the harnessed horse and shook his head. "Guess you're not taking us for a ride after, old friend."

The horse whinnied with apparent relief as Sampson undid the harness. Joanna shuffled in place, eager to get going but she wouldn't leave Sampson out in the barn on his own, not with his coughing fits that came so unexpectedly.

While she waited, she thought of the surprised look on Eli's face when she finally handed him the box. She just knew she was right, she had to be. The daffodils were the answer.

Chapter Ten

Seek and Ye Shall Find

When the horse was safely returned to its stable, Joanna waited for Sampson at the door. "I'll make sure you're safely on the porch and then I'm going back to the woods."

"What?" Sampson asked in surprise, moving towards her. "I might be sick, but I'm not an invalid."

"Sampson, you're tired."

"I might be, but I'm not dead yet. Let me just grab something first." He summoned a smile and started walking towards a storage closet. After searching for a while, he came up with two lanterns.

"We'll be needing these," Sampson announced before he started walking towards the woods. Joanna considered arguing with him, but he seemed set on going, whether she liked it or not.

Five minutes later Joanna and Sampson were heading back towards the woods, following the same path they had walked less than an hour before. Armed with lanterns and an extra shovel for Sampson, they kept walking as the sun slowly began its descent.

"Honestly, Sampson, there is no need for you to come," said Joanna. "Are you sure you're up to it?" She looked with concern at the thin man who was trying to keep pace with her.

"I can't let you go into the woods on your own, can I?" Sampson insisted. "It will be completely dark in less than an hour. You could easily get lost in those woods on your own, or be injured," he continued, drawing deep breaths. "Besides, I'm curious as to where this mystery box is that you have been searching for. I'll be fine, honestly."

Joanna knew he added the last part for her benefit because the concern was clear in her expression.

"*Denke*," Joanna whispered, half embarrassed by his kindness. He should be in bed, recovering from his sickness, but instead he was escorting her to the woodland to keep her from danger. She couldn't help but feel ashamed of all the bad thoughts she'd had about him over the last couple of weeks. He might not be the man she wanted to marry but if Ruth Beiler was willing, he would make a very good husband.

They passed the tree line that marked the start of the woods and almost immediately lit the lanterns. The thick covering of the trees caused it to be a good deal darker within the woods than in the field. As they walked through each clearing on the way back to where they had met that afternoon, Joanna swept her light quickly around each one to confirm her suspicions.

"At the risk of sounding completely foolish, what are you doing?" Sampson asked with a frown.

Joanna laughed, giddy as she began confirming her suspicions. "You'll see." She called over her shoulders as she rushed ahead.

Every single tree she had checked was the same. Instead of the thin grass or moss covering, each one was surrounding by budding daffodils. As for the clearings…they had nothing but a few clumps of moss and grass.

Behind her she heard how Sampson was tiring by his labored breathing, and she slowed down to wait for him. "You doing all right?"

Sampson nodded, his eyes wrinkling with a smile. "Just promise me you'll bury me where you find the box."

Joanna laughed shaking her head. "You're a nice guy, Sampson, it's a shame I don't like you in that way. Come on, I promise I'll plant a daffodil over your grave as well."

Together they walked through the underbrush, carefully watching as they walked. The last thing they needed was to trip, drop a lantern and start a forest fire.

After what felt like hours, but had been only about thirty minutes, they finally reached the clearing Joanna had been working in that afternoon.

At first glance there was nothing different about

this clearing, but if you knew what you were looking for...

A smile spread across her mouth as her eyes lit up with joy. There was one very clear difference if you looked closely enough.

She pointed excitedly. Almost in the middle of the clearing, just off the center, was a clump of daffodils. It was the same clump from which Sampson had picked Joanna's flower.

"It's there. Buried underneath that clump of daffodils. I just know it!"

Sampson frowned, dragging a hand through his hair. Clearly tired and very confused by her excitement. "How can you possibly be so sure?"

Joanna smiled triumphantly, "Not one single clearing has flowers growing in the center. I didn't notice that..." she trailed off as she started towards the daffodils. Without any reservations, she began to dig out the daffodils by hand setting them aside before reaching for the shovel.

"I have been digging in these woods for days now..." Joanna continued as she buried the shovel deep in the dirt. "This is the only clearing that has daffodils not growing at the base of a tree. How would those bulbs have gotten there? They had to have been moved."

"Are you sure?" Sampson asked, moving closer to light up the area around her.

"*Jah*. My guess is that when Eli buried his box all those years ago, this clearing was a whole lot smaller. With the many droughts since then, a lot of the clearings have expanded as some of the trees died." She paused for a breath while she collected her thoughts.

Because the clearing was smaller, Eli was burying it on the edge of the tree line back then. Just like he said he did. Then when he filled the hole in with soil from around the base of the trees, he transferred the daffodil bulbs with it. If you look around all the other clearings you will see flowers at the base of all the trees, there must be hundreds of bulbs around the edge of this clearing alone."

Sampson spun around, guiding his lantern to pick out the base of the trees. Joanna was right; virtually every tree had daffodils growing at its base.

"I just have one question. If there was a tree year eight years ago, where is it now? If it died, surely the stump would still be here."

Joanna shook her head as she smiled up at him. "Sampson, what do we use for firewood? Where do we find the wood?"

Sampson frowned before he began nodding, "Dry stumps in the woods. Someone obviously collected it for firewood…that's *if* you're right."

"I am right. I just know it. You finding me in the woods, giving me that daffodil…everything today worked according to *Gott*'s plan. That little memory box is just beneath this dirt."

He walked over to her, "I'm the *mann*, I should be doing the digging."

"Hush!" Joanna laughed. "You've probably done

too much as it is. You just catch your breath and hold that lantern steady so I can see."

Joanna drove her shovel into the soft earth and felt it hit something hard, as the sound of a shovel hitting wood reached her ears.

She looked at Sampson and smiled. "Told you!" she said triumphantly and then got down on her hands and knees and cleared the soil away with her hands. She reached down and pulled out a small wooden box. She very gently blew off the remaining dirt and stroked the box along the grain as though it was the most precious object in the world.

"I can't believe you found it," said a stunned Sampson, shaking his head in wonder. "Not only are you pretty, but clever too."

Joanna couldn't speak; her throat was clogged with emotion knowing how much this would mean to Eli. She held the box close to her chest and took a deep breath. The air was clean and smelled of pine and freshly turned dirt. She knew in that moment, she would remember the scent for the rest of her life.

She knew that this was *Gott*'s doing. She had been faithful, and although at times she had had doubts, she always ultimately believed that *Gott* would provide. She spent a moment offering a silent prayer of thanks. She stood up and wiped her dirty hands on her apron.

Turning to Sampson she offered him a grin. "Actually, you found it! If you hadn't given me that daffodil, it would never have come to mind."

Sampson smiled at the praise that he knew wasn't justified.

"Come on then. We need to take this back to Eli," she said.

"What? You're not even going to open it?" Sampson asked in disbelief. "You've spent days, weeks, searching for it and now you're not even going to see what's inside? I withdraw my compliment; you're not as clever as I thought."

Joanna laughed, playfully knocking his shoulder with her dirty hand. "*Nee*. It's not mine to open." She looked up and met Sampson's gaze and knew today she had found a friend. "This is something Eli should do on his own."

It was a private box, full of private, treasured memories. Who were they to open the box and intrude in such a way?

Sampson nodded in understanding. "Then let's get it to him."

Joanna was in a hurry to get to Jacob's farm, but she couldn't walk as fast as she wanted to. After almost a month in bed, Sampson was very weak, especially after the day's exertion. She kept her pace slower until they were barely moving, and then he began to cough fitfully.

Putting the box on the ground, Joanna went to him and gently patted his back until the fit was over. "Sampson, are you alright, shouldn't I get help for you?"

"*Nee*, I'm fine. We'll just take it slow," Sampson pleaded.

She didn't understand the pride some men took in keeping up appearances. There was nothing to be ashamed about when you were recovering from pneumonia, but she wasn't going to argue. Instead, she slipped an arm around his waist and guided him over the uneven forest floor. When he stumbled again, Joanna caught him just before he fell.

"There now, we're almost there."

Through the thick trees she could barely make out the dim light shining from the Stoltzfus kitchen. Every step they took was a step closer to Eli and a step closer to getting Sampson home.

They cleared the forest and stepped into the field where Sampson stopped to catch his breath. When he looked at her this time, humor was shining in his eyes.

"That *Englischer* better appreciate you, you'll make him a very *gut* wife."

Joanna laughed although her mind was filled with concern. She couldn't be anything of Eli's while he was still considered by the community to be an *Englischer*. As they crossed the field, she quietly prayed that this box would hold the answers that Eli was so desperately seeking.

When they arrived at Jacob's home, Sampson was huffing for breath, pale and very tired. "You sit down before you keel over," Joanna said firmly before turning to the door.

Too tired to argue, Sampson sat down in a rocking chair to her left.

Joanna knocked twice and crossed her fingers

that Eli would be home. She would feel horrible for dragging Sampson all the way there only to discover that Eli wasn't even home.

"I wish I was a little more presentable," Joanna whispered to Sampson, looking down at the dirty handprints on her apron.

"I don't think he will care. Truly, I don't," grinned Sampson. "I think the only thing he'll be focused on is the box in your hands."

Delia answered after a few moments with a look of slight surprise. "Oh! I was rather expecting somebody else. Joanna? How can I help you?"

"Is Eli home please, Delia? I've got some very exciting news for him," Joanna said, expecting the familiar shape of Eli to appear at Delia's shoulder at any moment.

Delia shook her head, grief making her look years older than her true age as she sighed heavily. "I'm afraid you just missed him."

"Missed him?" Joanna asked, confused, as Sampson stood up and joined her.

"Hullo, Sampson," Delia greeted a little confused before turning back to Joanna. "He left, Joanna. This time I don't think he'll be coming back."

"What?" Joanna wasn't sure if that was surprise or horror in her voice, she had a feeling it was both. "But it can't be, he would have…he would have said goodbye…"

Tears burned the back of her eyes. It felt just like eight years ago, finding out Eli had left without even saying goodbye. Her heart clenched in her chest as the first teardrop fell onto the wooden chest in her hands. Surely he would not be so cruel as to leave for a second time without speaking to her first. Would he?

"When did he leave? Did he tell you why? Surely he wouldn't have left without just cause," Sampson interceded, slipping a reassuring hand over Joanna's shoulder as he spoke with Delia.

Delia sighed heavily and brushed away a tear of her own. "The last week…he just hasn't been himself. Jacob tried to talk to him, but he wouldn't let up. A few hours ago, he arrived home, he had the look of a wild boar on his face and began chopping wood like there was a storm coming. Then suddenly he came into the house and charged up to his room. Jacob and I were both concerned, but before we could find out what was going on, he came out with all his belongings packed." She took a deep breath and shook her head. "He said that coming here was a mistake, that it would be best for everyone, especially for him, if he just left for Harrisburg."

Joanna listened but she couldn't seem to focus on anything but the pain blooming in her chest. Her fingers tightened around the chest, her white knuckled grip hurting, but she couldn't seem to let go.

"Why was coming here a mistake?" Joanna muttered almost to herself.

"Because of you…" Delia trailed off in barely more than a whisper. "I'm sorry. I didn't want to say this but I'm going to. It's none of my business how you run your life but leading on one man while engaged to another, it's ludicrous, Joanna Lapp."

Sampson squeezed Joanna's shoulder. "It's all been a misunderstanding, Mrs. Stoltzfus. Joanna and I aren't engaged. We just came from explaining to my parents that we don't want to proceed with the wedding they had all arranged quite against our wishes. It was never our plan to start with. Do you know which route he would have taken?"

The door opened wider and Jacob stepped out. He glanced first at Sampson and then at Joanna before tenderly lifting her chin to look him in the eye. "He mentioned something about needing to gas up before he drove back to Harrisburg. Might be if you hurry, you could catch him there."

Joanna shook her head knowing that all was lost. She finally found the box and now she would never have an opportunity to tell Eli. "It will take too long... I won't make it."

"Nonsense," Sampson said firmly from beside her before turning to Jacob. "Would you mind if we borrowed your buggy? I assure you that both your horse and buggy will be returned in the same condition in which we receive them. If we go back to my *haus* first, we'll never make it."

Joanna turned to Sampson, surprised that he was taking control of a situation that didn't really affect him in the least. "Sampson, you need to get home."

"*Nee.* We said we finish this today, we'll finish it. Mr. Stoltzfus?"

Jacob laughed shaking his head. "Why do I have

a feeling that if we bring Eli that box and the girl, he won't be leaving anymore."

Sampson smiled, "That's the plan."

A few minutes later, Joanna sat squashed between Jacob and Sampson with the box on her lap. The horse carefully trotted out of the yard as Joanna prayed that they would make it to the gas station in time. She didn't know much about how long it would take to refuel a car, but right now she hoped it took longer than the two miles they needed to ride to reach him.

She turned and saw Sampson's drawn expression and his labored breathing. She felt simply terrible for involving him in all of this, but she couldn't seem to make him understand that it wasn't his problem.

"Stop looking at me like that," Sampson mused with a smile as soon as he finished coughing. "Might need another week's bed rest after today. Probably a good thing we're not getting married, don't think I'll survive it."

Joanna laughed shaking her head when she saw the gas station in the distance. Only one more mile to go.

"Come on, Dale, almost there," Jacob urged, tugging on the reins.

Joanna held her breath as the cool evening air began to lick at her face. She glanced at Sampson, concerned about the cold on his chest, but she had told him he didn't need to come.

She saw a few cars at the gas station but couldn't be sure if Eli was still there. Besides the fact that she had no idea of the color of Eli's car, she couldn't tell any of them apart, anyway. As far as she was concerned there were two black cars, three white cars, a red car and one of those strange metallic blue ones.

Her heart jumped into her throat wishing him to still be there as Jacob guided the horses into the gas station. He pulled on the reins and the horses came to a stop, and then he turned to Joanna.

"He has a black car, not sure of the make and model but I know it was black." He shook his head while adjusting his hat. "Should've taken a closer look for all those weeks it stood in my barn."

"Joanna, go!" Sampson encouraged her.

She took a deep breath and handed Sampson the box before climbing out of the buggy. She turned to take the box from him, but he was already climbing out. "Sampson, stay where you are, it's getting cold."

Sampson shook his head with a smile. "How many times do I have to tell you…:"

"*Jah, jah*, but get moving. I can't miss him if I'm this close."

They rushed to the closest black car where Joanna noticed a woman seated behind the wheel only moments before she attempted to pluck the door open. Feeling foolish they walked to the next one. She peeked inside only to find that no one was inside the car.

A heavy feeling made her stomach drop as she turned to Sampson. "I think we missed him."

Sampson's smile broadened as he shook his head. "*Nee*, we didn't. He was in the convenience store."

He nodded his head at the exit just as Eli walked out. Eli looked dapper in a pair of jeans and a white knitted jersey. His eyes were cast to the ground, the frown on his forehead clear as Joanna and Sampson waited for him beside the car.

He looked up and their eyes met. For a moment her world tilted on its axis, knowing this was the man she wanted to spend the rest of her life with. A smile broke on her face even as her heart skipped a beat.

"Eli?" she asked, still holding the box.

But Eli didn't notice the box or the joy in her smile, all he saw was Sampson. "Am I getting a personal farewell from you and your fiancé?" he asked through clenched teeth.

Joanna frowned, anger rushing over the joy as she shook her head before she remembered his reason for leaving. "*Nee*, you don't deserve a personal farewell. Not from me, my fiancé, or anyone else. Not if you're going to be like that."

Eli laughed wryly. "How should I be, Joanna? Should I be overjoyed that you and Sampson have found happiness after your parents forced you into a relationship? Or should I applaud the fact that he's finally out of his sick bed?"

"Eli, you're being ridiculous!" Joanna snapped as he reached for the door.

Sampson stepped between them and shook his head. "Sorry, I don't mean to interfere, but you're not going anywhere until she's said her piece."

Eli turned to Sampson, squaring his shoulders.

Joanna flinched, the last thing she needed was for them to fight, with Sampson already tired and weak. "Knock it off, both of you."

Sampson shrugged. "Just trying to help."

Eli laughed. "Haven't you helped enough, already?"

"I don't know what you mean but this has got nothing to do with me." Sampson shook his head and gave Joanna a firm look that implied she'd better start explaining what was going on.

Eli glanced over her shoulder at the buggy. "You made my uncle drive you? Can't you even arrange your own buggy?" Eli asked Sampson with disdain.

"That's enough!" Joanna shouted. The anger and frustration in her voice sounded strange even to her own ears. She continued in a softer voice. "Eli…"

Chapter Eleven

The Explanation

Eli sighed. It was hurting him more than he cared to admit to see Joanna with Sampson at her side. What hurt him even more was that he could see just how much Sampson cared.

"What, Joanna?" he asked.

"This was the second time that you were going to leave without saying goodbye!" Joanna said coldly, her relief now mixed with a touch of anger.

Eli hung his head, unable to look Joanna in the eye. How could he have gone to say goodbye if he knew he wouldn't have been honest? He couldn't wish her a happy life, not with Sampson. Not after what happened that afternoon. But he didn't want to leave on the wrong foot.

"I'm sorry. I should have come to say goodbye. That was wrong."

"You're telling me!" Joanna replied quickly. She

grabbed his hand and pulled him away from the car and Sampson. She kept walking until they were out from under the fluorescent lights that illuminated the parking lot and the fringe.

"What happened, why did you decide to leave?" Even though the anger and disappointment were clear in her voice, Eli could see the love there as well.

He sighed heavily and shook his head before meeting her gaze again. "You chose him, Joanna…" the words trailed off. It was the first time he said them out loud and they still hurt more than he could imagine. "I couldn't stay here and watch you marry someone else. How am I supposed to accept that? You're the woman I've always dreamed of. You're the person I want to spend the rest of my life with. Instead, I packed up and did what any normal person would do—get out of dodge."

Joanna's brows rose slightly before they settled into a frown. "What do you mean I chose him? I've never chosen him. It's always been you. Just you…" She reached for his hand and squeezed it gently.

Eli withdrew his fingers almost as soon as their hands touched. "But I saw you? I saw you coming out of the woods together. You were laughing and carrying a daffodil. I don't have to be Amish to know that when a boy gives you a flower, he's courting you." He sounded caustic even to his own mind as he spoke the last words, but that was how he felt.

Joanna shook her head and a smile slowly began to curve her mouth. "Eli, you *dummkoppf*. I didn't choose him, not for a single moment. *Jah*, he did give me the flower but not as a gesture that we were to court."

"But..." Eli trailed off. "I saw you together." He shook his head wondering what she was playing at. He had seen the way they looked at each other. He'd seen the way Sampson had smiled at her when she draped her arm around his waist. She had to be lying.

"Eli, if you're not going to let me finish, then what's the use of this conversation?" Joanna asked before he could continue. "Just hear me out, alright?"

Eli didn't know if he wanted to hear what she had to say but if she had come all this way to stop him, surely he could waste a minute before he headed back to Harrisburg and his *Englisch* life. "I'll be quiet."

"I was in the woods this afternoon, digging for your box. Sampson found me in a clearing, furious that I was meeting you in the woods."

"But we weren't..."

"Hush!" Joanna laughed. "He thought that I wanted to marry him but was secretly meeting you in the woods every day. He watched us from his bedroom window. Can you imagine? He saw us both walk into the woods at different times and just accepted we were courting. So, this afternoon he followed me, he wanted to catch us, you see?" She shook her head still surprised at all the events that had transpired that day. "Anyway, after accusing us of all manner of improprieties, he finally gave me a chance to speak, and in a moment of pure anger I told him the last thing I wanted was to be engaged to him anyway. Do you know what happened then?"

Eli shook his head and Joanna smiled, knowing he was going to like her story from here. "He admitted he didn't want to marry me either. He's courting Ruth Beiler, you see. But before he could tell his parents that a match with me wouldn't work, he caught pneumonia, and everything spiraled out of control from there. After laughing about the horrible misunderstanding, we finally both agreed that we weren't suited to each other. That's when he gave me the daffodil."

"I'm still following…" Eli said. That explained why they had come out of the woods together, but it didn't explain why he saw them rushing back into the woods later that afternoon.

"We went back to his parents and explained to them that we didn't want to get married after all. We both expected a ruckus, but instead his parents understood. They actually didn't fight us on the matter. Sampson was kind enough to agree to speak to my parents as well, even though he was tired after being in the woods for so long. Just as we were about to head to my parents in his buggy, the thought hit me."

"What thought?" Eli asked, confused even more. This story seemed to have no end.

"Where you buried the box."

Eli's eyes suddenly widened. "You mean you found it?"

"Not just me, Sampson helped. We went back into the woods. This time with lanterns and an extra shovel…" Joanna's eyes brightened.

Eli nodded at the news, but he had just realized something much more important. The box wasn't what he needed in his life; what he had needed all along was Joanna.

"Enough about the box, I have something I need to ask you, Joanna. And this time I need you to be honest. This isn't about what your parents want, what Sampson wants or anyone else. I want to know what you want."

Eli watched her swallow before she blinked slowly. "*Nee*, Eli, before I tell you that, I need to know what you want."

Eli took a deep breath and stepped closer, taking Joanna's hand. "Ever since I could remember, you've been my friend. The last thing I expected when I came back to Lancaster County was to find you. But I did… Joanna, you've given me my faith back, you've taught me that there is joy in this world even if I've experienced so much loss. I want you, Joanna, but I can't have you if you don't want the same things."

"I want you too, Eli. I've never fallen in love with anyone because I always measured them against my memories of you. They were old, faded memories, but they were the memories I cherished." A laugh escaped her as she shook her head. "I fell in love, in the middle of the woods, knee deep in the dirt. I fell in love with a *mann* I barely knew. An *Englischer* my parents wouldn't approve of, but in my heart, I know it's always been you, Eli."

"I love you, Joanna Lapp," Eli whispered as he noticed a tear slip over her cheek.

"Will you stay if I say I love you?" Joanna whispered back, her voice cracking with emotion.

Eli nodded. "Even if you don't love me, I'm staying until you see your mistake. I'm staying, Joanna. I'll see the bishop, I'll go through a proving period, and I'll do anything it takes to be part of this community again."

Joanna smiled, shaking her head. "This day could have ended so differently."

Eli couldn't help but laugh, "I could've been halfway to Harrisburg by now if you hadn't caught up with me."

"Lucky Jacob knows how to drive a buggy." She laughed, referring to Jacob teaching him how to drive a buggy again.

"What about your parents, Joanna? I don't want them to hate you for loving me."

Joanna's eyes widened. "*Nee*! Sampson. He needs to get home. Don't worry about my parents; we'll explain it to them. Besides, he's in love with someone else." She waved the concern away even though Jacob could see it was troubling her more than she wanted to admit.

"Then let's get him home," Eli said, falling into step beside her. They headed to the buggy where

Sampson was sitting beside Jacob. "*Denke* for bringing her."

Leaving his car in the parking lot, they climbed into the buggy, squeezing in so everyone would fit.

"Your car?" Jacob asked, concerned.

Eli shrugged, "I'll have the dealership fetch it in the morning. I don't need a car anymore." With that he smiled at Joanna, knowing his future had just begun.

"Well, you're driving then!" said Sampson.

"My pleasure. Can I squeeze in there? You'd better move that, whatever it is, I don't want to break it." Eli pointed to his own box that sat forgotten on the seat.

"Oh," shouted Joanna. "I forgot!" She grabbed the box and held it tightly to her chest. "When I was in the woods today. I wasn't there without a reason. I found your box."

"What?" said Eli, amazed that Joanna did that for him.

"I've been searching for days. Today when Sampson gave me the flower, I finally figured it out." She held out the box. "We found it, actually. I'd never have thought of it without Sampson." Eli stared at the box unable to move. "Go on, take it," Joanna insisted.

Eli reached out, dumbstruck, and gently prized the box out of Joanna's fingers. He stroked the top as though he was cradling a newborn baby. "Both of you found this?"

"Yes. You know that daffodil you saw me holding this afternoon?" Joanna said, watching the tenderness with which Eli held the box. "Well, Sampson picked it for me out of a clump in the middle of a clearing. There were no other daffodils in the clearings in the woods. They were the only ones. When you buried it all those years ago, you must have moved the bulbs with it, it suddenly dawned on me. And when I dug there, that is what I found."

Eli laughed and shook his head. He looked up to the sky "*Denke, Gott*," he muttered. "It is almost unbelievable. Yet here it is."

"What?" Joanna demanded, looking confused.

"*Gott* sent me a sign. He sent a dream that I should seek out yellow flowers and the box would be there. It seems that you two found the right flowers."

"Are you going to open it?" asked Sampson, desperate to see inside.

Eli fingered the clasp, about to prise it open. And then stopped.

"What's wrong?" asked Joanna.

"Nothing," said Eli, stroking the top of the box again. "I'm not going to open it."

"What?" Sampson spluttered.

"No, you must," Joanna insisted, nodding her head in encouragement.

"*Nee*. This box is my past," Eli said, looking at Joanna. "I have my future right here. Opening this box isn't going to bring my *daed* back. He still lives where it matters. Here in my heart." He placed the box over his chest. "I thank you both for finding it. I really do. But I think that tomorrow I shall go and bury it again. And then I will look forward to my future."

Chapter Twelve

A New Day

The next day was a whirlwind of excitement and activity for Joanna. After arriving home so late the night before, both her parents had been concerned about her whereabouts, and rightfully so. She had told them what would hopefully prove to be her last lie, that she had lost track of time during her visit with Sampson. She was delighted when her parents didn't question her further.

After dropping Sampson off the night before he had promised to come and see her parents today so that the matter of their engagement could be cleared once and for all. Of course, Joanna kept a lookout at the kitchen window the entire morning while she helped her mother bake.

Although she wasn't a third of the baker her mother was, she enjoyed helping. There was very little in housework as soothing as watching butter and sugar blend into a smooth and creamy texture before adding it to the flour.

It was shortly after ten o'clock when she saw the King's buggy approach. Her heart jumped into her throat as she set down the mixing bowl. "Mamm, we seem to have company," Joanna said, pretending to be surprised.

"Ach *nee*, just look at the state of me. I'm covered in flour and sugar and, oh dear, there's even some frosting on this apron. Call your *daed* from the barn."

Joanna nodded before walking out the back door. After summoning her father from the barn, she quickly headed into the house just as there was a knock at the front door. Relief washed over her when she saw it wasn't just Sampson, but his parents as well.

After the formalities were dealt with and tea was served, everyone sat down in the living room, the only place that wasn't currently covered with flour in the Lapp household.

"I'm so sorry, if I'd know you were coming, I wouldn't have baked…" her mother trailed off apologetically.

Mrs. King waved her hand in the air. "We should have sent word, but alas we're here now and it is best we talk about this so that the matter can be settled."

"David, do you have something on your heart?" Jared asked his friend.

Joanna crossed her fingers, hoping they weren't

going to expect her to do the talking. She didn't feel as brave this morning as she had the day before.

"*Jah*, Jared, we do. It's come to our attention after frequent visits between our *kinners* these last few days," Mr. King glanced at Joanna and she wanted to kiss him for covering for her in that moment. "These two *kinners* aren't compatible. Our *seeh*, although eager at the beginning of this whole situation, has learned he has affections for another young girl. I won't name her, but I will say this, and I hope you agree—years, even decades ago, matches were made to prevent inbreeding and for other matters such as the gender ratio imbalance in certain communities. Today is very definitely not those times, Jared. We got caught up in the idea of becoming a *familye* without even considering whether these *kinners* were up for marriage in the first place."

"I wouldn't put it that way."

Beatrice shook her head as she reached for Joanna's hand. "He's right, Jared. Joanna made it clear to me that she wasn't interested in marrying Sampson, but I told her to abide by our wishes because that's what a *dochder* should do. I didn't once consider that Sampson might feel the same way as she does about the arrangement that we all made without considering their feelings."

"Well then," Mr. King stood up and stretched before smiling at the Lapp family. "I guess we can all put this behind us now and leave our *kinners* to find their own partners. I know that your *dochder* is a wonderful girl and would make any fortunate *mann* a very good wife some day. I hope you can trust in her judgment when that day comes."

Joanna caught Sampson winking at her and suppressed a smile, wondering if he had asked his father to add in that last bit as well.

"I will. We raised her with a *gut* head on her shoulders," Jared said proudly before turning to his wife. "Beatrice, don't you agree?"

"Of course. I hope your *seeh* finds love and happiness, David."

"*Denke. Gut* morning to you." David tipped his hat and after the greetings were done, the King family left.

Joanna hadn't moved, she sat rooted to the spot waiting for her parents to object or complain.

"What a relief," her mother said finally.

"I know," Jared sighed, relieved.

"What?" Joanna asked, confused. "I thought you wanted me to marry Sampson?"

They shared a look before Jared turned to his daughter. "*Jah*, we wanted you to marry Sampson but at the end of the day your happiness is more important to us. We could see you weren't happy with the decision, but I also couldn't go back on my word to Mr. King."

"A man's word is his honor." Joanna nodded as a smile spread across her face. "*Denke* for understanding."

"Nothing to understand," her mother assured her. "We were wrong all along."

With one disaster averted, Joanna now had another to solve. Her parents might be alright with the Kings breaking the engagement, but she didn't think they would be alright with her being courted by an *Englischer*.

A lot of things had to happen before Eli was a fully-fledged member of the community again and she didn't dare give her parents any cause to dislike him any more than they already did. Instead, she headed to the kitchen to help her mother bake and wondered when she would see him again.

Last night had been so confusing, so overwhelming, neither had arranged to see each other again.

But they had promised to spend the rest of their lives together. For now, that was more than enough, Joanna thought as she began beating the eggs into the sugar and butter mix.

Chapter Thirteen

Burying the Past

Eli walked through the woods, the box carefully clutched against his chest. This time he would mark the spot in which he buried it, he thought as he carried the shovel in his other hand. On top of the box was a rock on which he had carved his father's name and the dates of his birth and his death. It wasn't a tombstone, they didn't allow for that in Amish country, but it he could use it to mark the spot.

He found the clearing that Joanna had described to him and kneeled in front of the freshly turned earth. Before reopening the hole, he went to the base of a tree to scoop up a fresh batch of daffodil bulbs. Daffodils would mark the spot along with the rock, he thought to himself as he began to dig.

He had been searching for his happiness in his past for so many years; he never once thought to look to his future. Only now that he knew he would have Joanna with him did he realize the past didn't matter. His parents had been taken from him at a younger age than most, he had lost too much too soon, but he had also gained. He had gained the love of a wonderful woman. He had regained his faith, and all going well this afternoon, he would have regained his standing in the community as well.

Eli tucked the box safely into the ground before covering it with dirt and the daffodil bulbs. In his own way he was burying his worries and concerns along with the past. When he was done, he placed the rock on top of the freshly turned earth and said a quiet prayer.

He had two more stops to make before he returned to Jacob's farm. Two more stops that would in their own way determine whether or not he would be heading to Harrisburg later that day to finalize his life in the city.

Once he was finished, he brushed the dirt off the plain clothes he had worn that morning. At first it felt strange, the cotton wasn't as smooth, the shirts were a little scratchy, but this was who he was. This was who he was meant to be. Nothing had ever felt more right than that moment when he had placed a wide brim hat on his head.

He was Amish. Always had been. Although he had been away from his roots for eight years, they just needed a little faith to make them re-establish themselves. And faith was where he was headed next.

He took the buggy because walking would take

too long. With his uncle's permission and directives, Eli set off towards the bishop's house. The bishop's house was at the edge of the community, a little way away on the outskirts of town. Eli couldn't help but be nervous as he headed in that direction. Whatever the bishop said was the law in Lancaster County and if the bishop didn't permit him to stay, then he would have no other choice but to leave.

He couldn't imagine Joanna ever adjusting to an *Englisch* community and wished for it not to come to that.

He pulled up in front of the bishop's house shortly after eleven. Since he didn't have time to send word of his imminent arrival, he hoped the bishop would be home. Just as he climbed down from the buggy, the front door opened and the man in question stepped out. "Eli, I was expecting you to come."

The bishop smiled but Eli frowned. "Did you receive word?"

"*Jah*, from *Gott* more than a year ago." The bishop laughed at his own wisdom and took a seat on the porch. "More than a year ago I dreamed that you were coming back. I dreamed of you struggling through a very hard time before you came to see me."

"You mean like a premonition?" Eli asked, a little shocked as he stepped onto the porch.

The bishop shook his head. "It wasn't a premonition. I think *Gott* was just preparing me to be welcoming when you eventually arrived back where you always belonged. What can I do for you today?

I see you're wearing plain clothes, so I take it you're not here to say goodbye?"

Eli chuckled, shaking his head. "*Nee*, Bishop. I've come to ask your permission to stay. I know my situation is somewhat complicated, being that I left before *rumspringa* and without having been baptized, but I trust in your guidance as to how I can make this work."

The bishop nodded, carefully stuffing tobacco into his pipe. He slowly lit it before taking a deep drag. Very few of the Amish men still smoked, but the bishop insisted it was the only reason behind his good health. Eli didn't think it was his place to preach to a bishop about the proven dangers of smoking, such as emphysema and cancer.

"Well, it is a difficult situation, as you say. I can't merely baptize you, because I don't even know how strong your faith is. Faith is to be tested and tried like any good tool. Has your faith been tested, Eli?"

Eli nodded, a wry smile on his mouth. "More than I can say. But I can also tell you that it waivered. It waivered for a very long time, Bishop. I only found it again when I came back."

"*Gut, gut.* That's a start. You have been living the *Englisch* way for the last eight years, Eli, I expect you have matters in the city that you need to deal with before returning?"

"I do," Eli agreed. "I have an apartment, a job, a car. My household belongings that I need to deal with. If you're willing, I was hoping to head back to the city later today to handle all those matters."

"Let's do it this way, then," the bishop sighed and put out his pipe. "You can return to the community, but you will have a proving period. It won't be as long as a newcomer's, though…"

Eli's eyes widened. If an *Englischer* joined the community, their proving period could be up to a year. He didn't want to wait that long before he would be allowed to marry Joanna. "How long do you have in mind?"

"You've been staying with Jacob and Delia for the last month, so let's say three months from the day you return from dealing with your affairs in Harrisburg."

Eli nodded, relieved. Three months he could work with. "Will I be baptized after?"

The bishop laughed, "Why, are you in a hurry to court someone?"

For a brief moment Eli considered denying it but decided against it. This man was going to be as much a part of his future as Joanna was, it was best he was upfront about it. "*Jah*. I've fallen in love with Joanna Lapp. You can trust me when I say that I haven't courted her, we've only happened upon each other a few times. I know she feels the same way about me. I can promise you that I will not court her in any way until the day I am baptized."

The bishop sighed before shaking his head. "Does Joanna's father know of these affections you harbor for his *dochder*?"

"*Nee*. I wanted to come and see you first before I speak with her *familye*. I don't want to become part of the community under any false pretenses. I want to be honest."

"That's a *gut* way to start a new life. You have my blessing. Three months, Eli."

Eli thanked the bishop and slowly walked down the porch steps.

He could only wish for Joanna's father to be as accommodating as the bishop.

At exactly one o'clock, Eli stepped onto the porch of the Lapp home. His heart was pummeling to a steady beat in his chest as he knocked on the door. This meeting was the most important of all. He knew that Joanna's parents would be home for lunch and hoped he didn't ruin their appetites.

"What are you doing here?" Jeremiah asked with a smug look as he opened the door.

Eli swallowed his irritation at the wayward teenager. "I've come to speak with your father, is he home?"

"*Daed! Englischer*'s here to see you," Jeremiah called over his shoulder before closing the door in Eli's face.

He took a deep breath and prayed that Joanna's father would be more mildly tempered than his son. He waited a few moments before he heard footsteps approaching the door. The door opened and Jared Lapp stepped out with a frown creasing his brow.

"Good afternoon, Mr. Lapp. I hope I'm not interrupting your meal?"

"You're not, but if you were five minutes later, you would be."

Eli nodded and rubbed his damp hands against his plain black trousers. "Mr. Lapp, I was wondering if I might have a word with you in private. Mrs. Lapp is welcome to join if you wish, but I'd rather Jeremiah isn't present."

"And Joanna?" Mr. Lapp asked as a frown creased his brow.

"She's welcome to join us."

Mr. Lapp nodded and headed into the house. A few moments later Joanna and her mother joined him as they all gathered on the porch.

Eli took a moment to take in Joanna and felt his heart leap in his chest. This was the hardest conversation he was ever going to have but he knew in his heart it was worth it. Just looking into her beautiful eyes, he knew that she was worth every hardship he had to face to court her.

"Mr. And Mrs. Lapp, I've just come from the bishop," Eli suppressed a smile when he saw surprise dawn on Joanna's face. "I've asked to rejoin the community. The bishop agreed to give me a few days to deal with my *Englisch* affairs in Harrisburg before I return. When I return, I'm to have a proving period of three months."

Joanna's mouth tilted into a smile, and her father's brows concocted into a frown. "How is this any concern of ours?" he asked brusquely.

Eli nodded, "Because, Mr. Lapp, I told the bishop this as well. When my proving period is over, and I have proved myself a worthy member of this community and have been baptized—I plan on courting your *dochder*."

Mrs. Lapp gasped at his announcement; Joanna smiled but quickly adjusted her face before she looked for her father's response.

"You won't make three months," Jared Lapp said sternly.

"Oh hush, Jared," Mrs. Lapp said happily. "The boy is trying to tell you he loves your *dochder* and that he will do whatever it takes to prove that to us." She shook her head and turned to Eli. "Eli, once you're baptized, you're welcome to court our *dochder*." She quickly turned to Joanna with apology in her voice. "I'm sorry, dear, that's up to you to decide, isn't it?"

Joanna's smile finally broke through. "I'll welcome it, *Mamm*."

"*Gut*. Have you had lunch yet, Eli?"

Eli wasn't sure if he should kiss her feet or plead for her husband to stop glaring at him like a cradle snatcher, but it was Joanna's smile that made him smile. "*Nee*, I haven't."

"Then you'll join us, won't you?" Mrs. Lapp asked, turning to her husband. "He's welcome, right, Jared?"

Eli couldn't help but smile as Mr. Lapp finally nodded and opened the door. "You're welcome, but only to our food. You'll only be welcome to my *dochder* once you've been baptized."

Joanna laughed as her parents walked into the

house ahead of them. She turned and smiled up at Eli. "You've had a busy morning."

"That I have. I haven't thanked you for finding the box. *Denke*, Joanna. I buried it again this morning, in a place where I'll find it whenever I want to; but I realized that box isn't my future, Joanna, you are."

Her eyes filled as she reached for his hand and squeezed it tightly. "And you're mine. Let's go eat before my *daed* changes his mind."

With laughter in the air they walked into the kitchen. Even Jeremiah seemed to brighten a little and seemed for all the world to have stopped being rude.

Surrounded by Lapps, Eli knew that he couldn't wait for the rest of his life to begin, because with Joanna at his side nothing could scare him anymore.

Not even the thought of heading back to Harrisburg without her.

Chapter Fourteen

The Baptism

Three days in Harrisburg was more than enough time for Eli to sort out his personal matters. He cancelled the rental on his apartment, sold his car and most of his belongings, only packing what little he would need for a long life in Lancaster County.

It was also more than enough time for him to realize that he was making the right decision. In a city in which he had grown up and lived for all his adult life up to this point, he now felt out of place. There were too many people, there was too much noise and although he once called them friends, he didn't even feel sad when he said his goodbyes and farewells.

Lancaster County was his home now.

The money he made off of selling his belongings was donated to the bishop to use for whatever he felt the community needed. Apparently the one-room schoolhouse desperately needed a fresh coat of paint and some new chairs, and the church buggy was in dire need of repairs.

Not even when he had bought the latest flat screen television two years ago did it feel so good to spend the money, Eli realized the day he handed over the cheque to the bishop.

The next three months flew by in a whirl. Although it was his proving period, it felt to Eli as if he had already proved all he needed to prove. He knew how to be Amish and regaining his faith had been the best part of all.

He no longer sat in Sunday sermons wondering what the fuss was about; instead, he sat there and felt as if *Gott* was speaking to him directly. He didn't see as much of Joanna as he had initially hoped, but he knew that would change today.

This morning he would be baptized as a fully-fledged member of the community and if all went well, tonight he would be taking the girl of his dreams on their first buggy ride together.

The ceremony was longer than he had expected, but the message was clear. That even the prodigal son could return. Even the prodigal son deserved forgiveness and acceptance if he repented and proved himself to be worthy.

A typical baptism comprised a group of young people. Today it only encompassed one. When Eli was called to the front of the service, he stood up with heavy legs. He had dreamed about this moment for so long that, now that it was about to happen, he couldn't imagine what it would feel like.

When he reached the bishop, he answered the questions asked of him. One by one, he promised to be faithful to *Gott*, community and *familye* for as long as he should live. The bishop baptized him and kissed him on both cheeks before asking him to turn around as a fully-fledged member of their congregation.

Eli turned around and his eyes caught Joanna's gaze just as the tears began streaming down her cheeks. He knew the moment was just as important to her as it was to him. It was in this moment that the promise was made that their lives would be blessed. It was in this moment that he was returned to the community from which he had been torn when his *mamm* had suffered her own great loss.

After the ceremony he was overwhelmed with congratulations from everyone, but he couldn't seem to find Joanna anywhere amongst the well-wishers. After lunch, he went in search of her, but he still couldn't seem to find the woman he so desperately loved.

Doubts circled his mind. Did she cry because she didn't feel the way she declared at the gas station all those months ago? Had she fled before he could seek her out? He could also not find any members of the Lapp *familye*. Disappointed, he ate his lunch with Uncle Jacob and prayed that *Gott* would bring her heart back to him again.

Epilogue

Joanna accepted Jeremiah's offer to take her to the singing. If everything went as planned, she would have a buggy ride home. If not…she'd walk.

Shortly after the service just as they stepped out of church, her mother complained of a headache. Joanna had been about to offer her mother a cup of tea when her mother nearly fainted.

The entire Lapp *familye* was naturally concerned and agreed it was best for them to take her home. Joanna had searched for Eli but couldn't find him anywhere. Not wanting to delay the return home any longer than necessary, she joined her *familye* in the buggy.

The entire day, while she cooked lunch and tended to her mother, she prayed that Eli had not got the wrong impression from her early departure. Although neither had said anything, it was an unspoken given that tonight would be their first buggy ride together. Her father had insisted she go even though her mother was still feeling a little faint.

Concern had plagued her all day until her mother had called her to her room late that afternoon. It wasn't that she was plagued by illness, her mother had explained. Instead it was the life growing inside her. Joanna had been filled with surprise, excited at the idea of her parents finally having the third child they had been praying for for such a long time.

Once her mother explained that headaches and fainting spells were simply natural in the first few months, she too had insisted that Joanna should go to the singing.

She climbed out of the buggy and bid Jeremiah farewell as she walked towards the large barn. The singing was being held at the King's home tonight and Joanna couldn't help but be just a little curious whether Sampson and Ruth Beiler were finally courting.

She caught sight of them standing by the doors talking quietly and couldn't stop the smile that spread across her face.

But she didn't see Eli anywhere. Fear clutched at her heart at the thought of him misunderstanding her disappearance after his baptism, and then she saw a buggy approach. There was no mistaking that it was Jacob's horse that whinnied when Eli finally stopped.

Shyness and propriety forgotten, Joanna rushed towards the buggy just as Eli climbed out.

"Eli!" Joanna called out, rushing to him.

Eli's frown transformed into a broad smile. "You came!"

Joanna laughed. "Why wouldn't I, silly? We've been waiting for tonight for three months."

"But this morning after service…"

Joanna shook her head. "When are you ever going to learn to hush so I can explain?"

Eli shrugged, "I'm listening."

"*Mamm* was feeling faint; we needed to get her home. Guess what, Eli?"

"What?" Eli asked, mirroring her excitement.

"*Mamm*'s pregnant."

Eli laughed, "That's *gut*, I suppose. Are they happy?"

"Of course. A *kind* is a blessing from *Gott*, they're over the moon."

Eli stepped forward and took her hand in his. "So am I. Will you ride home with me tonight, Joanna Lapp?"

Joanna smiled squeezing his hand. "I'll ride with you for the rest of my life, Eli. I love you."

Eli's face broadened into a wide smile. "Then I take it the proposal has been taken care of. We'll just court for a couple of months to prove to your parents that I'm worthy."

Joanna laughed again, shaking her head. "No need to prove anything. Why do you think I'm here? *Mamm* and *Daed* insisted I come. Jeremiah even gave me a ride."

Eli laughed, surprise shining in his eyes. "Then, shall we go attend our first singing? If I drive you home tonight, I'm sure there will be no objections if I proposed tomorrow."

Joanna shrugged as she fell into step beside him, still holding his hand, "I thought the matter of the proposal has been settled."

Her heart soared as she noticed Sampson smile at her as they approached the barn. Beside him stood Ruth Beiler who was clearly infatuated with him. She still couldn't believe how wrong she had been about Sampson. There was a time when she despised him, and now he had become a good friend. A friend she knew she could rely on when things became tough.

She glanced back at Eli and a smile curved her mouth. A wedding…

Who would have thought that a mere four months ago she had thought her life was doomed, only to realize that *Gott* had been behind the wheel the entire time? She just had to be patient to see her intended destination. She smiled at Eli and knew that he would be her destination for so long as they both should live.

"So, have you thought where we're going to live yet?" Joanna nudged him with her elbow.

Eli shrugged, "Uncle Jacob's barn is quite roomy."

"Eli!" Joanna cried out in disbelief.

"I moved into my parents' cottage. The one on the other side of Jacob's property. It's been empty for years but I've been getting it back into shape."

"The one where you lived before?"

"*Jah*, I thought it was time that cottage was filled with laughter and love again."

Joanna sighed contently. She couldn't have thought of a better place to live. Now she just had to think of the wedding, her dress, the wedding date...

But none of that mattered; all that mattered was that she would be saying yes to Eli.

* * * * *

Anna
3/9/21

What on earth?

Suddenly, a shiny red Mustang came around the curve of the driveway at a speed far too fast for the dirt road, and when the vehicle slammed to a stop, it nearly hit the side of Avery's SUV.

Who drove that way, especially on unpaved mountain roads?

The man unfolded himself from the driver's seat and stood to his full over-six-foot height, let out a whoop of pure pleasure and waved his black cowboy hat in the air before combing his fingers through his thick dark hair and settling the hat on his head.

Avery had never seen him before in her life.

It wasn't so much that they didn't have strangers occasionally visiting Whispering Pines. Avery's own family brought in customers from all over Colorado who wanted the full Christmas tree–cutting experience.

So, yes, there were often strangers in town.

But this man?

LIEXP1220

He was as out of place as a blue spruce in an orange grove. And he was on land she intended to purchase—before anyone else was supposed to know about it.

Yes, he sported a cowboy hat and boots similar to those that the men around the Pines wore, but his whole getup probably cost more than Avery made in a year, and his new boots gleamed from a fresh polish.

Avery fought to withhold a grin, thinking about how quickly those shiny boots would lose their luster with all the dirt he'd raised with his foolish driving.

Served him right.

Just what was this stranger doing *here*?

"And didn't you say the cabin wasn't listed yet?" Avery said quietly. "What does this guy think he's doing here?"

"I have no idea how—" Lisa whispered back.

"Good afternoon, ladies," said the man as he tipped his hat, accompanied by a sparkle in his deep blue eyes and a grin Avery could only categorize as charismatic. He could easily have starred in a toothpaste commercial.

She had a bad feeling about this.

As the man approached, the puppy at Avery's heels started barking and straining against his lead—something he'd been in training not to do. Was he trying to protect her, to tell her this man was bad news?

Don't miss
Opening Her Heart *by Deb Kastner,*
available January 2021 wherever
Love Inspired books and ebooks are sold.

LoveInspired.com

HARLEQUIN

Heartfelt or suspenseful, inspiring or passionate, Harlequin has your happily-ever-after.

With new books published
every month, you are sure to find the
satisfying escape you know you deserve.

HNEWS2020

Love Harlequin romance?

DISCOVER.

Be the first to find out about promotions,
news and exclusive content!

Facebook.com/HarlequinBooks

Twitter.com/HarlequinBooks

Instagram.com/HarlequinBooks

Pinterest.com/HarlequinBooks

ReaderService.com

EXPLORE.

Sign up for the Harlequin e-newsletter and
download a free book from any series at
TryHarlequin.com

CONNECT.

Join our Harlequin community to
share your thoughts and connect
with other romance readers!
Facebook.com/groups/HarlequinConnection

HSOCIAL2020